Totally Bound Publishing books by Hannah Murray

Perfect Taboo

The Shame Game

Collections

Naughty or Nice?: Santa Daddy

Sun, Sea and…: Sun, Sea and Satisfaction Guaranteed

Perfect Taboo

THE SHAME GAME

HANNAH MURRAY

The Shame Game
ISBN # 978-1-83943-988-9

Interior text design by Claire Siemaszkiewicz
Totally Bound Publishing

Published in 2021 by Totally Bound Publishing, United Kingdom.

Totally Bound Publishing is an imprint of Totally Entwined Group Limited.

THE SHAME GAME

Dedication

I need to express my thanks and deep appreciation to fellow author J.S. Wayne. The information and insight he gave me on erotic humiliation and all the variations thereof was invaluable, and this book wouldn't be what it is without him. Any mistakes made are mine alone. Thanks also to the beta readers who gave their time to help me make sure I did justice to James and Amanda's story And to my husband, who kept reading even when his boundaries got pushed.

Content Notes from the Author

This book explores a kink known as Erotic Humiliation. While these themes may be uncomfortable or triggering for some, I want to assure you, my valued readers, that James and Amanda's journey of discovery is made with care and love, and with the full and enthusiastic consent of all parties. And while the emotional stakes of exploring a new kink are always high, this book was written to be a low angst, high heat journey that ultimately strengthens and enriches an already established relationship between two people who love each other deeply. I hope you enjoy their journey as much as they do.

If you'd like more detailed content information that may include spoilers, they can be found for this and all of my books on my website, www.hannahmurray.net, on the Books page.

Thank you for reading!

~Hannah

Chapter One

A dirty mind is a terrible thing to waste.
~ *Ouiser Boudreaux,* Steel Magnolias

James Douglass walked through the front door of his home and sighed with relief. "Thank Christ that's over."

Behind him, his wife let out a snorting laugh and shut the door. "You say that every year."

"I mean it every year." He turned to watch her slip out of her coat, the soft faux fur he'd given her for Christmas gleaming under the light of the foyer chandelier. "Tell me you don't feel the same."

Amanda smiled as she hung up her coat, then held out a hand for his. "I like your mother."

He dropped the bags he held and shrugged out of his overcoat. "It'd just be nice to be able to spend one New Year's somewhere else."

"Well, that's your fault for being born one minute past midnight on January first." Laughter colored her voice, deepening the Texas accent that still lingered more than a decade after she'd left the Lone Star State. "If you'd stayed put for another week like you were supposed to…"

"Oh, so now it's my fault for being born early?" He raised an eyebrow, wondering if his wife of twelve years would respond with sass or respect. He figured the odds were about seventy-thirty in favor of sass.

She took his coat with a wink. "Pretty much."

"Insolent wench," he muttered, and stifled a grin when she rolled her eyes. *Sass it is, then.*

"You could always tell your mom no when she invites us," she pointed out.

He sighed and bent to pick up the bags. "No, I can't."

"I know." She closed the closet with a snap and crossed to him, her bootheels clicking on the tile, and rose on her toes to plant a smacking kiss on his chin. "That's because you're a big old softie."

The eyebrow went up again, almost of its own volition this time. "What was that?"

"Sorry," she said, not looking sorry at all, her dimples popping out even as she lowered her eyes respectfully. "You're a big old softie, *sir*."

"Better," he allowed, fighting a smile of his own. "But you're lucky my hands are full."

She glanced down at the bags he still held, then back up at him, her brown eyes dancing. "Oh, yes. Thank goodness for those two duffel bags, otherwise I'd be in so much trouble."

James gave a bark of laughter. Apparently, he wasn't the only one tired of being on his best behavior for the last couple of days. "If I didn't know better, I'd say you were looking for trouble."

She walked past him, her dimples still winking. "Well, then it's a good thing you know better, isn't it? Besides," she continued, her voice drifting back to him as she moved toward the curved staircase. "Even if I was, it's not like you could do anything about it."

She paused on the first stair, her hand resting lightly on the banister, and looked back at him. They'd been together fourteen years, and still she took his breath away. Soft dark hair, a little tousled from the nap she'd taken on the drive home. Sparkling dark eyes, full of mischief and promise and affection. Her dimples flashed again, pulling his attention to her soft, full lips, curved in the faintest of smiles. That mouth had given him a jolt at their first meeting all those years ago, and its impact hadn't lessened over time. If anything, it had only grown stronger, because now he knew just what those lush lips were capable of. He knew just how swollen and red they grew from his kisses, how they looked wrapped around his cock. And how she bit them when she was in pain, or in pleasure.

Then those lips spread in an impish grin, bringing him back to the present, and the game she was trying to tempt him into playing. "It's not like you could chase me up these stairs or catch me even if you did. You're fifty-one now. An old man."

He growled because he knew she wanted him to, and with a rollicking laugh, she ran up the stairs.

He stayed where he was, enjoying the view. The yoga pants she'd worn for comfort on the drive home curved over rounded hips and a rounder ass, the soft sweater in misty green—another Christmas gift—covering bouncing breasts. He'd seen her dress that morning in a pretty lacy bra, the kind built for maximum visual effect rather than physical activity, so there was a lot of bounce.

It was pretty fucking hot.

He stayed where he was until she hit the top of the stairs and turned to look down at him. Even from this distance, he could see she was surprised he hadn't taken the bait. They'd been at his parents' house for three days, unable to play or even fuck the way they liked with his mom and stepdad sleeping down the hall, and only a few thin walls between them. A flash of uncertainty crossed her face, then it was gone, replaced by smirking confidence.

"Not up for a chase, old man?" she called, the mocking and teasing in her tone calling to him so strongly that he had to force himself to stay put. "That's fine. Why don't you go ahead and take those bags of dirty clothes to the laundry? Feel free to start a load. I'll just have a little reunion with my vibrator."

That nearly got his feet moving, but he was enjoying the anticipation too much. "You know the rules, little girl," he warned.

"Rules?" She smirked, leaning over the banister so her sweater gaped, giving him a tantalizing view of soft breasts and white lace. "Rules only count if you can enforce them."

Anticipation sang in his blood. "You're taking big chances."

A flicker of unease crossed her face before she smoothed it away. "You don't worry me," she called back, and only he would've heard the nerves in it.

"Oh, yes I do." He let his grin turn feral, loving the way her body tensed even as she sneered. "Because you know if I get up there and find you touching what's mine without permission, there will be consequences."

Her laugh was full of anticipation and apprehension, a heady mix that had him going rock hard in his jeans. "By the time you manage to drag your old bones up here, I'll have had two orgasms, a shower, and will already be asleep."

She gave a little toss of her head, sending her short sweep of dark hair flying. "Don't forget to start the laundry," she said, then disappeared down the hall.

James waited until the bedroom door slammed before he started up the stairs. He took his time, going first to the second-floor laundry room to drop off the bags. He set them on top of the washing machine where she couldn't miss them, then continued on to his home office. He'd told his clients he was taking the week off for the holidays, so there was nothing pressing waiting for him. Still, he checked his voicemail, and glanced at a set of blueprints that had been delivered just before Christmas. He frowned over them for a moment, jotting down a few ideas for his meeting with the engineer next week and making a note to ask his assistant to check that the soil testing at the site had been completed.

Then he set down his pen, shut off the lights, and walked down the hall to the bedroom.

The double doors were shut, the room beyond silent. He thought about giving her a few more minutes, to make sure she'd had enough time to get started, then shrugged. If she hadn't already begun to masturbate—strictly prohibited without permission, as she well knew—then he'd punish her for the threat of it.

Though their D/s dynamic was fairly flexible, and almost everything was open to negotiation, rules were rules. She liked to push from time to time, as though testing to make sure those rules were ironclad, and he liked to remind her that they were. He didn't mind her pushing—in fact, he'd be disappointed if she didn't. Just as she'd be disappointed if he didn't hold to the line they'd agreed on and punish her appropriately for crossing it.

He did so hate to disappoint his wife.

He rolled his shoulders and stretched his neck, loosening muscles that had grown tight on the long drive. There was always a chance he'd have to wrestle her down, and Amanda was much stronger than she looked. After three days of enforced celibacy, he was almost hoping she'd run.

He pushed open the doors.

The room was brightly lit, both bedside lamps and the chandelier above the bed glowing, banishing the shadows of twilight to the far corners of the room and spotlighting the woman on the king-sized bed.

She'd propped herself up, a pile of pillows at her back so she sat almost upright. Her clothes were scattered across the foot of the bed and the floor beside it, leaving her bare against the bright blue of the duvet beneath her.

He took a moment to drink in the sight of her, his beloved. Soft breasts, their weight resting gently on her ribcage, her reclining position widening the space between them so he could clearly see the small scar over her breastbone. Her nipples were still soft, pale brown puffs that would pucker and tighten as her arousal grew, and looked their best, in his opinion, when they were pinched in a set of clamps and glowing bright red.

Her belly was a soft curve, round hips flowing to firm thighs that he loved to dig his fingers into when he fucked her. The harder the better, so she'd see the bruises left behind the next day and preen a little in the mirror.

She spread her legs, revealing the soft skin of her inner thighs with their pale stretch marks and the tuft of dark hair at the top of her sex. She would have preferred to completely wax her pubis, but he liked having something to get his fingers into, so they compromised. She left the hair on her mound alone, the dark curls a wild tangle for him to play with, but her pussy below was stripped bare of hair. The soft pink flesh glistened in the bright lights, already slick with her own arousal and probably some lube,. because she likely wouldn't have been able to get the huge purple dildo wedged all the way inside her cunt so quickly without it.

He stared at the offending object for a moment, to increase both her unease and his control, then raised his gaze to hers. She was biting her lip, nibbling at it the way she did when she was unsure but was trying hard not to be, and her nipples were already hardening.

Aroused, and a little scared. Perfect.

"I thought I told you not to touch what's mine without permission."

She shrugged, a smirk on her pretty face despite the growing anxiety in her eyes. "Oops."

He had to fight to keep his lips from twitching. "Oops? You're going with oops?"

"Oopsie-daisy?"

He forced himself to frown. "Being cute won't save you."

"No?" She shrugged again, her tits bouncing enticingly with the movement. "I might as well enjoy myself, then."

She lifted her hands to her breasts, her short red fingernails gleaming against her skin. Her breasts were delightfully responsive, the nipples puckering and lengthening at her touch. She pulled them with her fingertips, her breath hitching at the contact, and he grew even harder.

"This might take a while," she said, her voice thin and tight with arousal. "I used the Velvet Swing."

His gaze darted to the bedside table, and the distinctive bottle that sat there. Velvet Swing—or the good lube, as they sometimes called it—was a cannabis-based lubricant sold by their local pot shop. Infused with both THC and CBD, it increased blood flow and intensified arousal, and often triggered Amanda into multiple orgasms. They tended to save it for those times when they wanted a long play session, as it required about forty minutes after application to reach full potency.

Apparently, Amanda wanted to play hard tonight.

"You have until the count of three to stop touching my property, Amanda," he warned her. "One."

She brought one hand to her mouth, sucking two fingers inside with a noisy *pop* that had him grinding his teeth against the surge of desire. "Two."

She pulled her fingers away from her mouth, sliding them down her throat and between her breasts, leaving a damp trail behind. She skimmed them across her belly, drifted past the thatch of pubic hair, to hover over her clit, out of its hood and clearly visible. He held his breath as she kept them there for a moment, teasing both of them, before she grabbed the wide base of the protruding dildo.

"Three," he growled, the word mingling with her reflexive moan as she shoved the dildo deeper into her pussy, and he was moving before the sound faded.

He was beside the bed in a heartbeat, and surprise lit her eyes when he lifted her into the air. She flailed in his arms, the dildo falling to the bed, and her laughing squeal was cut off abruptly when he sat on the side of the bed and pushed her face down over his lap. He planted a hand on the back of her neck to counter her instinctive attempt to right herself.

"You asked for this," he reminded her, and brought his hand down on her ass.

She squealed again, bucking against his hold, and he barely avoided a foot to the face. Fighting back a laugh, he shifted to wedge her legs between his, clenching his thighs to keep her in place, then shoved her face towards the floor. She grabbed his leg, digging her short nails in through his jeans as she pushed herself up.

He smacked her ass again, a short, sharp blow right on her sit spot. "Stay put," he ordered, and grabbed the dildo off the bed to unceremoniously shove it back into her cunt.

Her choked "Oh, shit!" was accompanied by a hard buck of her hips that would have resulted in her getting free if he hadn't had her legs trapped. He kept one hand firmly between her shoulder blades, holding her down, and worked the dildo with the other. Her pussy was tight, the way her legs were clamped together making for an even snugger fit than usual, so he took his time, pulling it out slightly, wiggling it a bit, pushing it back in. He thought about stopping for more lube, something slicker and more viscous than the cannabis cream she'd already applied, but he didn't want to let go of her long enough to dig into the nightstand drawer. Instead he slowed down the process, drawing it out so that by the time he had the dildo fully seated in her cunt, her thighs were slick, and she was panting.

"That's pretty," he observed, and gave the wide base of the toy a firm pat that made her hips jerk. He grinned at her upturned ass and did it again, her strangled moan delighting him.

"Tell me what you're getting a spanking for, Amanda."

"Because you're old?"

He tsked in mock disappointment and smacked the base of the toy again just to listen to her moan. "Try again."

"Because you have no sense of humor?"

Smack. "You're going to find out just where my sense of humor lives if you keep playing games. Last chance. Why are you getting a spanking?"

Her body tensed as she hesitated, and he knew she was weighing her options. She undoubtedly had another smart-ass remark dancing on the tip of her tongue, ready to launch, but she was also starting to realize the precariousness of her situation. They both enjoyed the punishment games that made up so much of their kink, but there were limits, and she knew it. She wanted to come, and knew that if she pushed him too far, he'd make his point by not letting her.

He waited for her to make her choice. If she chose obedience, he'd fuck her until they both came screaming. If she chose insolence, he'd put her smart mouth to good use for his own pleasure, then send her to bed, aching and wanting.

Either way would be fun for him, but he hoped she'd choose obedience. After three sexless days, he missed her, and he'd love nothing more than to give her as many orgasms as she could take before curling up to sleep with her wrapped around him, limp and satisfied.

But the choice was hers.

The seconds ticked by, and he was on the verge of reminding her there was a question on the table—via the forceful application of hand to ass—when she let out a resigned sigh. "Because I was masturbating without permission."

Relief and desire flooded him in equal measure. "And why do you need permission to masturbate?"

"Because my orgasms belong to you."

"That's right," he replied, and rewarded her by giving the base of the dildo a solid wiggle. "You put the lube on just before I came in?"

"A couple of minutes before, yes, Sir."

"Hmmm." He glanced at the clock on the fireplace mantel across the room. "Then we've got about half an hour before it really starts to kick in, don't we? Let's see if we can spend our time wisely. Count."

He lifted his hand, waited for her breathless "Yes, Sir," then let it fall on the fullest part of her upturned ass, making sure to catch the edge of the protruding dildo.

She jerked, moaned out "One," and he stroked his hand approvingly over the pink that had bloomed beneath his hand.

"Good girl," he praised, and, seeing that the dildo had begun to slip out, nudged it back into place. She was even wetter, the column of silicone sliding back in much more easily than it had even just a few moments ago.

Excellent.

He glanced at the clock, calculating how many swats she could take and still be in the right head space for what he had in mind. One smack every two minutes should do it, he figured, and, drawn out over half an hour, wouldn't be too taxing. And while he was counting down the seconds to the next spank, he could play.

Amanda had no idea how much time had passed. She knew it had been a while, because she was counting the spanks, and he'd just delivered number fourteen. James pulled her up by the hair every five smacks so some of the blood could drain out of her head. It also gave him the opportunity to play with her nipples, now clamped—he must have had the alligator clips on standby—for a few moments before he pushed her back down. But the lightheadedness wasn't so bad, and at least while her pussy was in the air, he was paying attention to it. At this point the lube was kicking in, her pussy swollen and engorged, tingling on the verge of a hard orgasm, and God, she wanted it.

Unfortunately, he didn't seem to be interested in making her come. He kept his touch light, even careless, every move seemingly geared toward reducing her to a mindless puddle of helpless lust. And it was working.

In between smacks—which *hurt*, dammit, he wasn't going easy at *all*—his fingers were busy, scraping over the heated skin of her ass, their calloused tips rough against the tenderized flesh. Gliding through the moisture that pooled between her thighs, drawing light circles around her clit and stroking over the stretched lips of her pussy, or tapping with a firmer touch on the slick pucker of her asshole. And slowly, too slowly to bring any relief whatsoever, fucking her with the dildo she'd so foolishly thought to tease him with.

If he didn't let her come soon, she was going to start drooling.

Well, she was already drooling, but since she was chewing on the leg of his jeans to muffle her moans, at least he'd be the one to have to deal with it.

She couldn't remember the last time she'd been this worked up. Her ass was raw, and little pulses of pain radiated from her clamped nipples. The chain that connected them was just heavy enough to act as a weight that pulled at them unceasingly—*thanks for nothing, gravity*—adding to both her distress and her arousal. Her pussy was on fire, pulsing and throbbing around the thick toy, and she'd swear she could feel her heartbeat in her swollen, aching clit.

The Velvet Swing might, in hindsight, have been a mistake. Sure, the orgasms she had with it were longer and stronger than the ones she achieved without it, and she could often count on having more than one, but none of that did her any good if he *won't let me come,* something she should've considered before putting her *tease James into a scene* plan into action.

She could only hope he'd be horny enough to put an end to this torture soon, but she knew from experience he was capable of denying himself for hours to draw out a scene.

She was contemplating all the ways she could grovel her way into an orgasm when his hand landed on her ass again, and sent her thoughts scattering.

"Fifteen," she managed, groaning out the count along with her frustration as need and pain burst through her. The blow was hard enough to rock her forward on his lap, making her breasts bounce and setting the chain connecting them swaying. Tension spiked, sharp and sweet, drawing another groan. Her hips rolled, a helpless, instinctive motion, her searching for relief. The dildo began to once again work its way out of her with the movement, and she flexed to help it along, needing the slick slide of the silicone against her swollen cunt. But instead of fucking her with it as he'd been doing for the last half hour, he pulled it free.

Surprised, she started to turn, and suddenly found herself being lifted up. The room spun for a moment as the blood rushed from her head, and by the time her vision cleared, she was flat on her back in the middle of the bed, almost in the same position she'd started in.

Oh, thank God, he'd decided to stop toying with her. No doubt the last half hour of play had aroused him, especially after three days at his mom's house. She sent him a smile, sure she'd find him shedding his clothes, preparing to climb on top of her and give her the solid fucking they'd both been craving. Instead, he was fully dressed and frowning at the bench that sat at the foot of their bed.

She watched, confused, when he pushed it away from the footboard. "James? What are you doing?"

"Who?" he asked, his voice hard, giving the bench a solid nudge with his knee, not even looking at her, and she felt the first real twinge of *uh-oh*.

She swallowed. "Sir, what are you doing?"

"Setting up the spectator area, of course," he replied. Apparently satisfied with its placement, he turned to face the bed and sat on the bench.

"Um." She swallowed, eyeing him cautiously. He was leaning forward slightly, silver-streaked hair tousled, his hands resting on his thighs. He seemed relaxed, at ease, until she saw his eyes. She'd been looking into those eyes for nearly fifteen years, and she didn't need the corresponding bulge in his jeans to tell her he was aroused. And she didn't need to see the slightly mocking curl to his lips to understand that she was in trouble.

She wiggled a little on the bed, wincing when her tender butt scraped against what she'd always thought was their softest duvet cover. He hadn't hit her much—fifteen was pretty light, actually—but the whacks he'd landed hadn't been gentle. "Sir?"

He jerked his chin. "Pick up the dildo."

She glanced down to see the purple dildo, still slick from her pussy, lying next to her. Heat seared her cheeks. She didn't know why, but seeing the evidence of her arousal on it brought a wash of shame that made her grateful she wasn't looking at him.

Confusingly, it also brought a flood of fresh desire.

Swallowing hard, she did as she was told, her cheeks burning hotter when she saw the damp stain left behind on the duvet. She glanced up again, forcing herself to meet her husband's gaze, and awaited further instruction.

His eyes had narrowed slightly, and she knew he hadn't missed her reaction. For a moment she thought he might question her about it, then he jerked his head. "Use it."

The quick rush of relief at not being questioned quickly burned away as she realized what he was asking. "Sir?"

"Use it," he repeated, relaxing even further on the bench, looking as though he was getting ready to watch a very boring, very predictable sporting event. "You were so eager to come that you decided to break the rules, so go ahead. Make yourself come."

She stared at him, shocked and more than a little thrown by the order. "What?"

"You heard me," he said, no softness or give in his tone at all, pinning her with those unflinching, icy eyes. "Fuck yourself with the dildo and make yourself come. Or," he continued in the same even tone, "don't come at all."

"Until when?" she blurted out, dismay making her voice squeak.

"Until you fuck yourself with the dildo and make yourself come."

Chapter Two

Amanda stared at her husband for a full ten seconds. Surely he wasn't asking her to do what she thought he was asking her to do? She kept waiting for him to laugh, tell her he was just kidding, then climb on the bed and fuck her, but he didn't. He just stared back at her, one dark eyebrow raised in his *I'm waiting* look, and she realized with a hard clutch in her gut that he was absolutely serious.

He'd never asked her to perform for him before. Okay, so every time they did role play it was kind of a performance, but that was different. That was a role, an act, and he was usually acting right along with her. This was her, and it was him, and even after fourteen years together—twelve of them married—the idea of putting herself on display for him made her feel nearly faint with embarrassment.

Which didn't make sense. It wasn't as though he'd never seen her naked or on display before—of course he had. When they played, when they fucked... Over the years he'd seen every part of her body, in nearly every state it could be in. He'd mopped up her vomit when she was sick, helped her use the toilet when she'd thrown out her back... It was impossible to be with someone for so long and not have the 'or worse' part of 'for better or worse' pop up now and then.

But none of that had made her feel like this, and she didn't know what to do about it.

The look in his eyes said she'd be doing as she was told, unless she used her safeword. She would if she needed to—he knew that, trusted that—but she didn't. She just needed to find a way past the stunned shock that he was really going to sit on the bench at the foot of their bed, the one she'd had reupholstered in deep gray when they'd redecorated, and watch her masturbate.

His eyes glittered, his expression clear in the bright lights. "Do I need to repeat myself?"

She was shaking her head automatically before the words had fully registered. Making James repeat himself was always a bad idea, and she tried to avoid it whenever possible, but she just couldn't seem to push through the quagmire of her thoughts to obey.

"No, Sir," she managed, her voice a ragged squeak.

"Then do as you're told."

Her hand was moving, obeying almost without her direction, bringing the dildo between her spread thighs. It had cooled, and she flinched at the first touch of it against her heated flesh, bumping her clit before sliding lower, through the soft, slick folds to her opening.

She dropped her gaze, unable to bear looking him directly in the eye for one more second, but the view between her thighs did nothing to cool either her embarrassment or her desire. The view was blurry without her glasses, but she could see enough. Her pussy was pink and wet, the folds flowered open to reveal her hard clit and the darker pink of her opening. She wished she was lying flat, without the pillows propping her up, because then she wouldn't have to see it, the purple of the dildo's molded head almost garishly bright next to her engorged flesh.

"Put it in," James said.

She did, holding her breath. It parted her inner lips, pushing through to the hole that waited, aching and empty. *Hole,* she thought again, the simple word somehow so fucking filthy that just thinking it brought a new flush of heat to her cheeks and a new rush of wetness to her cunt, and the dildo slipped inside.

"There you go," he said, his voice hard and impersonal, as though he were describing some detail of architecture on an old church, except he'd probably sound excited about architecture. "All the way."

She bit her lip and obeyed, working the toy as deep as it could go. She was wet, but the toy was thick and curved, and it took a while to get it into place. Her hand was wrapped around the flared base, fingers pressed into her swollen pussy, and she wiggled to get the last half inch seated. It was lewd and vulgar and so goddamn sexy, and even though the sight was slightly fuzzy without her glasses, she couldn't tear her gaze away.

"Look at me."

Only the hard note of command in his voice could've pulled her away from the mesmerizing display. She looked up immediately to find him watching her with that icy, impersonal stare.

Which, to her astonishment, made her pussy clench on the dildo. *Hard.*

"That's a greedy fucking hole," he said, his eyes locked on her pussy, his voice mild and matter of fact, as though he were discussing the weather or how he was thinking of buying a new sweater. "Isn't it?"

"Yes," she whispered, so turned on that pushing the word out felt like a herculean task.

"Say it."

"It's a greedy fucking hole," she parroted, shame breaking over her in a hot wave even as her pussy clenched again.

"Who has a greedy fucking hole?" he asked, still discussing the weather.

Her voice was an agonized whisper. "I do."

"Spread your legs wider," he said, and she did, fighting to breathe through the embarrassment. "Wider," he said again, and she brought up her knees and spread her thighs, a small whimper escaping when the dildo shifted inside her.

"You like that slutty hole stuffed full, don't you?" he said, his mild tone giving the words an unexpected punch. "You going to come?"

She whimpered again, shocked to realize how close she was to getting off. She hadn't touched her clit, wasn't moving the dildo in and out, the friction she normally needed to get there absent, and yet she could feel the orgasm coming. Her pussy throbbed, her nipples pulsed in the clamps, and James' impersonal stare made her whimper once more.

"Do it." He lifted his eyes from her stuffed cunt to her face, his expression almost blank, his gaze like flint. "You wanted to come, so do it. Come like the horny, cock-hungry slut you are. Put your fingers on that clit and rub it until you fucking come."

She obeyed, holding the dildo in place with one hand and moving the other to her clit, her eyes locked on his face. He sat on the bench, calm and unmoved by her ragged breathing or the way she jerked when her fingertips brushed her clit, his gaze not even flickering. He leaned forward, with his forearms resting on his thighs and his hands dangling between them, relaxed and loose as though he was just waiting for a bus that was late, slightly irritated by the inconvenience of it all.

"You're not rubbing it," he said, some of that irritation leaking through now. "If I have to come over there because you can't follow a simple fucking instruction..."

She sucked in a breath, a streak of fear lancing through her at the thought, and rushed to set her fingers on either side of her clit. She began to rub.

He shook his head, disappointment and disgust filling his eyes. "I said on it, Amanda, not beside it. Rub. Your fucking. Clit."

She shook her head. He knew how sensitive she was when she was this aroused. Direct contact on her clit would bring an orgasm, yes, but it would be as painful as it was pleasurable.

"Are you safewording?"

"No, but..."

"Then do it," he said, unyielding and unsympathetic, his gaze flinty, and his eyes shifted meaningfully for a long moment toward the wardrobe that housed most of their toys before returning to hers. "If I have to do it for you, you won't like it."

She swallowed hard, not wanting to give him any reason to get anything out of the wardrobe. Not the Hitachi, or the violet wand, or even a crop. In this mood, he'd choose the most diabolical thing he could find, and use it without mercy. She'd come screaming, but experience told her he wouldn't stop with her orgasm. Unwilling to test him, she braced herself for the jolt and set her fingers firmly on top of her clit.

The cry spilled out, jerked from her throat despite her best efforts to keep it in. The sensation that blasted through her was diamond bright, with sharp edges that stole her breath. Her clit felt huge under her fingers, scraped raw before she even began to rub, and the slight blast of pain seemed to shove her orgasm further away even as it made her want it more.

"That's it," he said, a hint of praise slipping into his tone. "Come on, fuck yourself with that fake cock, too, there's a good slut. Jam it into that greedy fucking hole as hard as you can."

She clung to that thin thread of approval and obeyed, pumping the dildo out and back in again, hard enough that she grunted under the impact.

"Keep going," he muttered, his voice guttural now. "I can see your cunt sucking that thing in. So fucking greedy, that pretty little hole. Take it out."

It took a second for the command to register, but then she tugged the dildo free, wincing when her cunt clamped down on it, blushing when it finally slipped out with a long, liquid sound.

And when he chuckled, she nearly came on the spot.

"Didn't want to give it up, huh?" he said lightly, just enough mockery in his tone to make her face flush hotter and her cunt clutch harder.

"Look at that." He leaned forward, his eyes riveted on her open pussy, and she obeyed.

Her cunt was bright pink, and so wet she could see it glisten in the lights. Her hole—*God, there's that word again!*—was open, the lips spread wide to accommodate the dildo. She felt it spasm, as though seeking the return of that penetration, saw it flex and pulse with blurry eyes. And she knew there was no way James could miss it.

"Fuck, yeah," he muttered, and her eyes flew to his face. He wasn't impersonal or impassive now. His eyes were sharp slices of blazing blue, and his cheeks had gone ruddy with color. His normally clean-shaven jaw was shadowed with a few days' growth of beard, and it was clenched, his teeth grinding, as he stared at her wide-open cunt.

She made some sound, a sigh or a whimper, and his gaze flew back to hers. "I can see everything, Amanda."

I know, she thought.

"I can see your pretty tits and your pretty face and your pretty, slutty cunt, red and wet and wide open, just begging for something to fill it up. Is that lube working?"

She blinked, thrown by the question, but apparently he didn't expect an answer because he kept talking.

"I bet it is," he continued. "I bet your pussy is going crazy, those little flutters and pulses getting stronger. I bet your clit feels like a ripe little berry, ready to split from the pressure. And I can see all of it."

He waited a beat, that little smile finally curling his lips, sharper and meaner than she was used to. She shuddered with both arousal and fear, and the smile sharpened some more. "Put it back in and fuck yourself until you come."

She brought the dildo, still in her hand, back to her pussy, pushing it in with ease now, her body accepting it eagerly, and began a swift in and out that quickly brought her lust back up to boiling point.

"Clit, too," he directed, and she moved the fingers that had stilled on her clit. Her hips jerked with every stroke, pain and pleasure like twin bolts of white-hot lighting.

"Keep your fucking legs open," he snapped, and she realized she'd brought them closer, the way she always did when an orgasm was imminent, as though she was trying to hold the sensation in. She fought to keep them spread, wishing he'd tied her down so she wouldn't have to struggle, but somehow the struggle made it better.

"Look at me, Amanda," he ground out, his voice a guttural growl now, and she had to fight to keep her eyes on him just as she fought to keep her legs spread.

"That's it, keep watching me. I see you, Amanda, your slutty little hole grabbing at that cock, wanting more of it. Keep your fucking legs open," he snarled, his lip curling into a sneer. "You don't get to hide from me. I get it all. You hear me? I get it all."

"Yes, I hear you," she gasped, the tension in her belly winding tighter and tighter, the pressure building. Her cunt was beginning to flutter, hips pumping as she jerked the dildo in and out.

"Say it." He leaned so far forward that his chin skimmed the mattress, his eyes glued to the pistoning dildo, to her frantically rubbing fingers. "Say it."

"You get it all," she managed, arching into the sensation, and broke on a wild cry. The orgasm rushed through her, bright and razor sharp, the rhythmic pulses of her cunt drawing hard on the toy, fueled by the cannabis lube and the stinging embarrassment of knowing he was seeing every bit of it. She forced her eyes to stay open, watching him watch her, and the satisfaction and possession stamped on his expression made the spasms start anew.

When they finally faded, she slumped against the pillows, her hand going slack on the dildo and her fingers falling away from her clit. Her breath came in ragged gasps, her skin damp with sweat as she shuddered out the last of her pleasure with her eyes locked on her husband's face.

His gaze lifted slowly from her pussy, skimming over her thighs, her breasts where the clamps still adorned her nipples—and now that she was coming down from the orgasm, they were *really* starting to hurt—to rest on her face. Her cheeks heated once again when she realized how she must look, her hair a wreck, and the light makeup she'd worn for brunch with James' parents probably gone or ringed around her eyes. She lifted a hand instinctively to fuss at her hair, to try to restore it to its usual sleek order. She froze when he barked out, "No."

Her hand hung in the air for a moment, hovering as though the message to lower it hadn't quite made it from brain to muscle, then it dropped, and her face burned hotter.

Why was this so *humiliating*? He'd seen her this way, a sweaty wreck from sex or a scene, too many times to count. So why was *this* time different?

A thought slipped into her mind, diaphanous and fleeting, gone before she could fully grasp it. Then James looked straight into her eyes and said, "Again," and every other thought flew right out of her head after it.

She'd had three orgasms and was working desperately on the fourth when James flicked his gaze to the clock on the mantel to check the time. Nearly an hour had passed since he'd ordered her to masturbate, and he figured he'd just about pushed her to her limit.

His wife was a flushed and sweaty mess. Her hair, normally a sleek, dark cap, stuck out in all directions, snarled and matted. Her whole body was sheened with sweat, the smooth, olive-toned skin bright red and patchy in places, and her cheeks were streaked with the little bit of eye makeup she'd put on that morning.

He wondered fleetingly how she'd look right now if she'd done the heavy smokey eye she liked to wear for parties, and made a mental note to make sure that happened at some point in the near future.

But right now, he had other fish to fuck.

He'd made her reapply the cannabis lube about half an hour ago, despite her very real distress at the notion. She'd actually begged him not to make her do it, which just demonstrated how far gone she was. He loved it when she begged, and had rarely in all their years responded to it with anything resembling mercy, so the fact that she'd been moved to beg while knowing perfectly well it wouldn't work was telling.

His poor wife was having a tough time of it, and it was only going to get worse, because as soon as she got herself off again, it was his turn.

He watched her fingers move over her clit, jerky and uncoordinated, while her other hand held the dildo planted deep. She wasn't even attempting to fuck herself with it, but he'd decided to let that go, knowing that at this point her cunt was so sensitive that the penetration alone was probably enough to keep her on the razor's edge.

Her pussy was a thing of beauty right now, swollen and red, the lips so puffy from the hammering dildo that they looked as though he'd been using a suction cup on them. Her clit was equally swollen, a bright red button at the top of her sex that he knew was causing her equal parts pain and pleasure. Pain, because it was so sensitive from the constant friction, and pleasure because she liked it when it hurt.

It was his favorite thing about playing with her. Or had been, until he'd seen how she reacted to the humiliation of masturbating in front of him.

She'd done it before, of course, but this was the first time he'd removed himself so completely from the scene, more director and observer than participant. A proportional punishment, he thought, for such a blatant disregard for one of their few fundamental rules. And since she had no doubt been expecting the spanking to be the end of it, it was a fitting way to remind her that he could—and would—administer those punishments according to his desires, not hers.

He loved that she loved being punished, or 'funished', really, since they both knew she was breaking the rules for fun, but he was still in charge.

Something she was being rather forcefully reminded of at the moment.

"Don't stop," he said, keeping his tone flat and his face passive. Not an easy feat, since his cock was so hard it hurt, and all he wanted to do was bury it inside her.

"I can't," she managed, her normally smooth voice a heavy rasp colored by exhaustion and pain. A strand of hair was stuck to her cheek, teasing the corner of her mouth as she stared at him with unfocused eyes ringed with what was left of her mascara.

"You will," he replied, projecting unfeeling detachment for all he was worth. "If you ever want to be allowed to come again, you'll come now."

Her fingers stroked over her clit again and her body jerked. Her whimper of distress had his cock hardening even further in his jeans. "I can't," she moaned, utter despair in the guttural sound. "Please, Sir. Please."

Every cell in his body was clamoring to stand up and rush to her, to lie down beside her and hold her close and whisper that she'd been such a good girl, so strong, so beautiful. Instead, he forced himself to sigh loudly, pushing disappointment and anger into the sound, and rose to his feet. "I should've known you'd need help," he said with a hint of derision, watching her face carefully for any signs of emotional distress at the words.

All he saw was relief, so he walked around the side of the bed, close enough that he knew she wouldn't be able to see him clearly without her glasses. He stripped, careful to keep his movements economical and unhurried—it wouldn't do for her to think him too eager. He toed off his shoes, kicking them to the side then unbuckled his belt and pulled it from the loops, flicking his wrist to make the leather *woosh* and *snap* as it came free. She jerked at the sound, then again when he dropped the belt onto the bed, her eyes following it down before jerking back up, worry in their soft brown depths.

He kept the smile from his face with an effort and continued to efficiently strip. Sweater, then jeans, followed by socks and boxer briefs. He took off his watch last, when her eyes were glued to his straining cock, and when he laid it on the nightstand, palmed a bottle of lube—the regular kind—and a condom from the open drawer.

He climbed onto the bed, careful to keep the items in his hand hidden, and settled himself between her spread thighs.

He jerked his chin at the dildo still wedged in her cunt, her hand still wrapped around the base, tightly, as though it were an anchor. "Take it out."

Her teeth sank deep into her lip and discomfort crossed her face as she obeyed. It was slick, both from her own arousal and the thick lube he'd directed her to use after orgasm number three, but her vagina was swollen and no doubt tender, the engorged lips clinging to the silicone shaft, and he knew if he fucked her pussy as hard as he wanted to, she'd likely be in some serious discomfort come morning.

It was good, then, that he had other options.

It came free with a slurp, loud in the quiet room. Her face was flushed again, her embarrassment at the inelegant sound clear.

"Nasty," he said mildly, testing. Her flush deepened, and she was looking everywhere but at him. "Look at me, Amanda."

The command in his voice had her gaze snapping back, her eyes filled with need and pain and the delicious sheen of shame that until today he'd have sworn he had no interest in seeing there.

Even after fourteen years, she could still surprise him.

"Are you going to come again or not?" he demanded, forcing himself to stick to the script. He was ready to finish the scene, to come himself then spend the rest of the evening taking care of his wife, but he wanted to do it right.

"I can't," she whispered, despair turning the words into a sob. "I'm sorry, Sir. I can't."

"I don't care," he said, and saw her eyes go wide with shock. He hadn't snapped or snarled, and somehow the words had even more punch without the force of emotion behind them. "Grab your legs and hold them back."

She obeyed, her hands sliding behind her knees automatically, though she still stared at him in shock. She pulled until her knees touched her breasts, wincing when they brushed against the clamps still on her nipples. He made a mental note to get them off soon, then returned his attention to her pussy, on full display between her open thighs.

"Look what you've done to yourself, Amanda," he said, forcing his voice to deliberate coldness when it normally would've vibrated with reverence.

God, she was beautiful. Red and wet, swollen and open, her cunt looked as though it had taken a serious pounding—which he supposed it had—and was eager for more. The little patch of pubic hair decorating her mound glistened, the hair matted in places from lube and sweat and the thick, slick wet of her come.

"What a greedy little fuck hole," he said in the same cold, impersonal tone. "It's still open, Amanda. You fucked yourself so hard I can see right inside you."

And he could, the pretty pink just inside her pussy on full, glorious display. He leaned forward, his hand wrapped around his dick, and slapped the swollen head against that pouty opening.

Her groan was like a song. He did it again, luxuriating in the feel of her hot, sticky flesh against his straining cock. Fluid drooled out of the tip, spattering on her bright pink labia with the next smack, and for a second, he thought about getting up to find his phone to capture it. But she was near her limit, and he wanted to come.

"I'm going to fuck you, Amanda," he told her, and, picking up the condom, used his voice to cover the sound of ripping foil. "I'm going to fuck you and you're going to come one more time, aren't you?"

She shook her head, her eyes glued to his face, not even noticing when he rolled on the condom. "I can't, I really can't."

"Then it'll be a very long time before you do it again," he reminded her, and watched her face twist in shame and frustration. He picked up the lube, making no attempt to disguise the sounds of the cap opening, or of the lube squirting out of the tube into his hand. He slicked up his cock, stroking it slowly, the sound of it loud and lewd. She relaxed fractionally at the sound, gratitude shining from her eyes, and he knew she assumed he was lubing up so he could make fucking her battered pussy more comfortable for her. He let her think it, let her relax even more as he added more lube. Satisfied it would be enough, he wiped his hand on her pussy and rose to his knees.

"Keep your legs back," he told her, letting his dick fall against her open cunt, smacking the tender flesh. He dragged it down, dipping the head into her open, gently pulsing hole a scant inch, just a tease, then slid it down to the slick, untouched pucker of her anus and grinned when her eyes flare wide with surprise.

"What, you didn't think I was going to fuck your cunt, did you?" He forced a laugh, watching her eyes, the set of her mouth for signs of distress or rejection. The worry that edged into her eyes didn't bother him—he'd be worried if she wasn't a little anxious. "I want a tight fuck, and that slutty hole is probably so wide open right now, I wouldn't even feel it."

She jerked against him as the words hit, and he thought for a moment that he'd gone too far. He waited, his heart in his throat, ready to pull the plug and spend the rest of the night apologizing at the first hint of a safeword. Then she said his name on a long, low moan, the way she always did when she was so worked up she couldn't remember to call him Sir any longer, and he knew she was with him.

He leaned into her, pressing his cock into her tightly puckered hole, grunting with satisfaction when it gave way. He slipped inside her an inch, then two, grunting again at the way the muscle spasmed around him, squeezing and fluttering as she adjusted to the invasion. He pulled out with a *pop*, watched her asshole flutter closed, then pushed inside again.

He did it several more times, going deeper and deeper with each intrusion, stopping to add more lube before going in again. Soon, when he pulled out, her anus wasn't closing all the way, staying open and ready for him to burrow back in, and he let out a low laugh.

"Another greedy little hole," he choked out, gritting his teeth. He slid all the way home this time, not stopping until his balls were pressed against her upturned cheeks. "That's what you are, isn't it? Just a collection of greedy little holes for me to fuck."

Her eyes were locked on his face, her asshole spasming around him. He leaned forward, shoving himself a fraction of an inch deeper, grinding his abdomen against her swollen, open pussy, just to make her do it again.

"Oh God," she whispered, her feet kicking into his shoulders as her ass flexed and pulsed on his dick. He knew he wouldn't last long at this rate. He could already feel the tickle along the base of his spine, in his balls. Determined to take her with him, he leaned back a bit when he pulled out, and set his hand on her cunt.

"No!" She jerked hard at the contact, but she was pinned down, and there was nowhere to go.

"Yes," he countered, and, determined to make her come one more time, shoved two fingers into her cunt.

"Oh *fuck*," she groaned. He pumped them in and out quickly, a counterpoint to the slow, measured advance and retreat of his cock. He stroked his fingers against his cock through the thin wall separating pussy and ass, and it was almost unbearably erotic.

He was close, too close, but Amanda wasn't.

"Put your feet on my shoulders and let go of your legs," he told her, grunting a little when she complied.

Her legs were strong from the gym and the half marathons she liked to run, and he knew she was fully capable of kicking him right off the bed if she chose.

He sank his cock back into her ass, just a little bit faster than before, and pulled his fingers free of her clutching pussy. He couldn't help smiling when she moaned in disappointment, then stiffened with renewed trepidation when he laid his hand at the top of her mound, just above her clit. "Put your hands on your tits and squeeze."

Her hands fluttered in the air for a second before she obeyed, her fingers spreading to cup each bouncing globe from underneath, avoiding the clamps, and squeezed lightly.

He shook his head. "Harder," he demanded, and slapped her clit.

Her scream rent the air, her hips jerking so hard she almost unseated him. If her ass hadn't simultaneously clamped down on his cock, she might have.

"I said, squeeze them harder," he ground out, and lifted his hand again.

"Don't," she begged, her hands squeezing much harder now, fingertips denting the soft flesh. "Don't."

"Good girl," he praised. He pumped into her ass a little harder and watched her breasts bounce. "What a good little slut you are."

Fresh color flooded her face, and he wondered briefly if she was pleased with the praise or embarrassed by it. Making a mental note to ask her later, he moved just a little bit faster, and kept talking.

"You like my cock in your greedy hole, slut?" he asked, grinding the words out as he thrust heavily into her. She nodded, sweaty hair flopping over her brow. "Say it."

"I like it," she gasped, her hips lifting into his jutting cock, and he knew she was starting to feel it.

"Say it all," he commanded, and, tangling his fingers in the thatch of sweaty, matted pubic hair, yanked.

"God!" Her hips shot up, desperate to ease the tension, and his cock sank even deeper into her. "God!"

"All of it," he repeated. He eased his grip slightly as his hips picked up speed. "Or I'll smack that fat little clit again."

"I like your cock in my ass," she said, her breath coming in desperate pants, her hips rolling up to meet his thrusts.

"That's not what I said, is it?" he snarled, twisting his fingers in the hair to pull the strands tighter and up, toward her belly button. The action tugged on the skin around her clit, his favorite way of working it without touching it, and though the action wouldn't do much, he knew it had done enough when she moaned. "Try again."

"I like your cock in my greedy, slutty hole," she wailed. "James, please!"

"Grab the clamps." He pumped his hips faster, racing now. He kept one hand planted on the mattress, digging his knees in for leverage, the other still tangled in her pubic hair. "Grab them, Amanda."

She fumbled to obey, her hands sliding on her sweaty breasts. She'd either have to pinch them to compress the spring and relieve the tension, or simply pull them off. Pinching was nicer.

"Pull them off."

"Please," she whined, her fingers poised on the ends of the clamps. "Please, let me pinch them."

"You disobey me on this, and I swear to God you won't sit down for a fucking week," he ground out.

She was breathing so hard it sounded as though she were sobbing, and her eyes pleaded wordlessly for mercy, but he had none. He was hanging by a thread, barely holding back his own orgasm, pounding into her now. Her ass was fluttering around him, her belly rippling under his hand as her orgasm built. The clamps coming off would hopefully send her over the edge, and as soon as they did, he could let his own release come.

"Amanda. Pull." *Thrust.* "Them." *Thrust.* "Off."

She sucked in a shuddering breath, her body tightening as she braced herself, then she yanked the clamps off her swollen nipples, and for a heartbeat, relief flooded her eyes. Then her gaze was full of pure, screaming agony as blood rushed painfully back into the abused little nubs, and her head went back on a cry and she began to come.

"Thank fuck," James breathed. Her ass clamped down, and he dropped his head and drove his hips forward, powering through the clenching muscles. Her left foot skidded off his shoulder and whacked him in the jaw, but he barely felt it. His orgasm seemed to come from his toes, rushing through his body in a tidal wave of sensation. His guttural groan escaped through gritted teeth as white-hot pleasure dimmed his vision and roared in his ears, and he emptied himself into the condom.

He hung there a minute, sweat dripping off his face to splash onto Amanda's belly, the room filled with his ragged breaths and her whimpering pants. His mind shifted sluggishly to what came next. He needed to pull out, get up and deal with the condom, then give her the aftercare they both needed. They'd need to talk about the scene, what they'd done and how they felt about it, but that could wait until morning.

He pressed a soft kiss to her sternum, gentle and sweet. "I'm going to pull out," he murmured, and waited until she managed a feeble nod before he moved.

He went as slowly and as smoothly as he could, but still she flinched. He petted her leg, her hip, whispering nonsense words of comfort, and quickly dealt with the condom. He stood, wincing a little when his back twinged, then turned to scoop her into his arms.

"Your back," she murmured, snuggling close.

"It's fine," he assured her, and carried her into the adjoining bath. "Tub or shower?"

"Tub," she said with a sigh. "But I have to pee first."

He carried her to the toilet, setting her carefully on her feet. When he was certain she could stand on her own, he left her there to take care of business and moved to the large soaking tub under the wide window.

He turned the water on hot and tossed in a handful of Epsom salts. The toilet flushed, and he turned back, eyeing her critically as she walked toward him. "All right?"

"Fine," she said, her voice soft. "You?"

"Right as rain," he said, and pressed a kiss to her hair. "I love you."

She tilted her face up at that, streaked with makeup and still blotchy from her orgasm. And when she smiled at him, she'd never looked more beautiful. "I love you, too."

"Come on, into the tub," he said, and nudged her along until they were lying together in the blissfully hot water. "What do you want for dinner?"

"Anything I don't have to cook," she replied immediately, and he laughed.

Chapter Three

James woke early, as was his habit, and slipped quietly out of bed. At just shy of five a.m. the sky outside was still dark, and at this time of year would be for a couple more hours. Normally he'd open the blackout curtains so that when dawn broke, the east-facing room would flood with light. Amanda claimed that it was easier to wake up when the sun was shining, but this morning he left them closed. She didn't have to work, and he wanted to let her sleep.

She'd had a rough night.

He glanced back at the bed where she lay sleeping, curled up on her side with the blankets covering most of her face, so the wild tangle of her hair was all that was visible. She'd slept heavily, only shifting position a couple of times in the night, a sure sign of exhaustion. The long car ride, plus what had turned into a pretty hard scene, had taken a toll, and she'd nodded off during the movie they'd put on after dinner.

He looked at her for a moment longer, before stepping into the bathroom. He took care of business quickly, then slipped back into the bedroom to gather a T-shirt and a pair of sweats, opening and closing the dresser drawers as quietly as he could, and carried the clothes with him into the hall.

With the bedroom door shut securely behind him, he dressed before taking the stairs to the main floor and heading for the kitchen.

The wood floors were cold on his feet, though he barely noticed. He went through the familiar task of pulling the gourmet coffee beans out of their canister and grinding them up. Amanda would want some when she woke, even without work on the agenda, and though he didn't drink coffee himself, he enjoyed the ritual of making it. He especially enjoyed doing it the morning after a scene, when he knew his beloved would be off kilter, and he could provide a small thing to help right her world again.

He measured the beans into the grinder and set it whirling, his thoughts doing the same. He hadn't intended for the scene to go where it had last night. They almost never played with erotic humiliation, though not because of any conscious decision to restrict it. It just wasn't part of their dynamic, which leaned toward the fun and performative. They liked role playing and costumes, and their scenes tended to be low stakes, at least emotionally.

That had changed last night.

He'd intended to have her masturbate for a few moments to finish off her punishment—which wasn't really a punishment at all, even though she *had* broken one of their few hard-and-fast rules. They'd been together long enough that a lot of their pre-scene negotiation happened in a kind of shorthand. If Amanda started acting the brat, the way she had last night, he could either shut it down or let it roll. If he let it roll, it was understood that what followed was all in good fun, and that no actual punishment would be forthcoming.

He hadn't shut her down, so she'd rolled with the bratty submissive character, and he'd rolled with her. At first.

He frowned and went over the scene in his mind, his stomach tight with unease. It had started out typical, the spanking and the teasing in line with how they usually played, but when he'd positioned himself at the foot of the bed and ordered her to masturbate, something had changed.

She'd looked embarrassed, and he'd known immediately it wasn't part of the role. Amanda was a good actress, but even an Oscar-caliber performer would have a hard time replicating the physical signs of humiliation. The flushed face and neck, the hammering pulse. The playful glint in her eyes had been replaced by nerves, even a little bit of fear, and that wasn't something he saw often.

It was so rare that he'd nearly called it off, but then he realized something else—it had turned her on. Her pupils had dilated, and her breathing had hitched the way it did when she was caught up. And then she'd obeyed.

It had taken all his discipline to keep from falling on her like a starving wolf.

He poured the freshly ground beans into the coffee maker, then crossed to the sink to fill the pot with water. He knew they'd need to discuss what had happened, how it had made her feel, but he'd held his tongue last night. Unless she safeworded out of a scene, or it had otherwise ended badly, Amanda liked to take her time processing. The things he was ready to talk about immediately—what worked, what didn't, how she felt, how he felt, and so on—she would need time to mull over. When it was clear that she'd been in a good place last night, he'd concentrated on aftercare, knowing that either this morning or later today she'd be ready to talk about it in depth.

He poured the water into the coffeemaker and turned it on, then crossed the open space to the living room. A flick of a switch had the gas fireplace roaring to life, filling the room with light and warmth. He chose a seat on the sofa, and while the coffeemaker burbled and bubbled across the room, picked up the book his wife had given him for Christmas and settled down to wait for her.

Amanda followed the glorious scent of coffee into the kitchen. She'd slept later than she'd intended—with the curtains closed, the bedroom was like a cave—but she didn't have to go to work until next week and neither did James, so she didn't care that she'd slept half the day away.

She shuffled into the kitchen, wrapped in one of James' robes, with a thick pair of socks on her feet to keep the icy hardwoods from assaulting her bare toes, and headed straight for the coffee pot.

The little clock on the machine was a glowing red blur, reminding her that she'd forgotten her glasses again. Annoyed that turning forty-six this year had apparently triggered what her younger sister liked to call Middle Age Vision, she grabbed a blurry mug from the blurry cabinet and filled it with blurry coffee.

A soft laugh from the living room made her turn to find her husband lounging on the sofa, an open book in his lap and a smile on his face.

"Forgot your glasses again, didn't you?" he asked, clearly amused.

She wrinkled her nose at him, sipping her coffee as she crossed the room. "I'm not used to them yet."

He raised an eyebrow and shifted his legs to make room for her. "You might get used to them if you actually wore them."

She leaned down to kiss him, then eased down beside him. "I don't want to get used to them," she grumbled into her coffee. "I don't think I really need them, anyway."

"You couldn't see me clearly last night."

She frowned, twisting her head to look up at him. And he was blurry, dammit. "Yes, I could."

"When I was sitting on the bench, sure. But you didn't see me get the condom and the lube from the bedside table, did you?"

She sniffed. "That's because I was dizzy from three orgasms, and you were being sneaky."

"I'm not that sneaky," he pointed out. "Admit it, I was blurry."

"Fine, you were blurry." She shifted around so her back was nestled into his side and pulled her feet up onto the sofa. "Happy now?"

"Thrilled," he said, and poked her in the side of the head with something hard.

"Hey." She twisted around, her frown deepening when she saw the glasses he held. "Where'd you get those?"

"Where you left them, on the end table." He wiggled them in front of her face. "Come on, be a good girl."

Muttering under her breath, she wedged her coffee cup between her knees and took the glasses. Not even under the threat of a single tail whipping would she admit that it was a relief to put them on.

"Good girl." He dropped his arm from the back of the sofa and wrapped it across her chest. She retrieved her coffee cup and snuggled into it. "Ready to talk about it?"

"Sure," she answered absently. She was marveling at the crispness of the writing on the side of the cup, a promotional item for one of the charities she worked with. Damn, she really did need glasses.

He tapped her nose with one blunt fingertip. "Amanda."

"Sorry." She twisted to look up at him. "I'm ready if you are."

"I was ready last night, but you wanted to eat Thai food and fall asleep during *Field of Dreams*." He closed the book and set it aside, then lifted her into his lap.

"That movie really drags in the middle," she said, balancing her coffee cup with the ease of long practice.

"Blasphemy," was his mild retort. "You want to go first?"

She settled into the curve of his arm, the cup cradled in her hands as she thought back to last night. "No physical problems to report. My pussy's a little sore, and so is my butt, but nothing major." She wiggled on his lap to demonstrate.

"Nipples?" he asked, stroking over the slope of one breast with the backs of his fingers.

She shivered a little at the contact. "No, they're fine. I've had clamps on for a lot longer than that before."

"True." He dropped his hand from her breast, sliding it across her belly to wrap around her hip, warm and solid. "What about the non-physical?"

She blew out a breath. "That was a lot."

"I know." He squeezed her hip. "Tell me about it."

"It all seemed normal until after the spanking," she said slowly. "Normal for us, I mean. Like a regular funishment scene."

He nodded. "To me, too."

"But then..." She shifted a little, twisting her hips so she faced him more fully. "When you sat on the bench, and you told me to masturbate for you..."

"It embarrassed you," he prompted.

"Yes, but that's not..." She blew out a breath, frustrated that she couldn't seem to put into words what she was trying to say. "You were just looking at me. And you were so far away."

His gaze softened. "It made you feel disconnected."

"Yes." She nodded, relieved that he understood. "Disconnected, and I guess unsure. I wasn't sure if we were still in funishment mode or not, you know?"

He nodded. "I can see that. How did you feel about the embarrassment?"

"I really liked it," she said, and it felt like she was confessing to a deep, dark sin. "And I kind of hate that."

"Why?"

Her throat felt tight, so she brought the cup to her lips for a sip before answering. "I don't think I would've been embarrassed if you'd been with me. On the bed with me or just touching me in some way, you know? But you were so far away, and I couldn't tell if you were happy with me or not, so I started getting anxious, and..."

"And what?" he prompted when she broke off, his voice soft. All the love and affection that had been missing from last night's scene was in his voice now, and it gave her the courage to continue.

"The words you used," she said, swallowing hard. "Slut. Greedy."

"Hole," he supplied, and she knew by the way her cheeks had heated that she was blushing again.

"That one especially," she said, her eyes focused on his chin. He was still sporting his vacation stubble, silver like the streaks in his hair. She frowned a little at a dark spot on his jaw. "What's that?"

"What? Oh." He stroked his thumb over the bruise. "That's where you kicked me last night."

She bit her lip to hide her glee. "I'm sorry."

"No, you're not." He raised an eyebrow. "You were saying?"

"Right." She cleared her throat, still staring at the bruise. "I don't know why, but every time you said it, I just cringed."

"And got hotter?" he asked, stroking her hip when she nodded.

"Lots hotter. It made me feel…not devalued, exactly, but reduced, in a way. Like all the other parts of me had gone away, and I was just that. Just a greedy, slutty hole." Her breath shuddered out. "And I liked it."

"I know. You came four times," he reminded her.

Her cheeks flamed hotter. "That was the cannabis lube."

"Some of it, but mostly, you just really got off on it. I did, too."

Her eyes darted up to meet his, surprised. "You did?"

"You couldn't tell?" he asked with a low laugh

"I could tell you were turned on," she said, babbling a little as she grappled with this new information. "But I wasn't sure about the rest. It was just so different from how we normally play, you know? I just wasn't sure."

"I liked it," he assured her. "I liked that it turned you on so much to be reduced to a greedy, slutty hole."

"I'm not sure I do."

"You've always liked dirty talk," he pointed out. "What is erotic humiliation but dirty talk on steroids?"

She frowned a little, rolling the phrase around in her mind. "I always thought of erotic humiliation as something, well, mean. Things like making a submissive be a toilet, or an ashtray, or something like that."

"I think it can be whatever you feel erotically humiliated by," he said, then shrugged. "But honestly, I don't know much about it. I'm a novice here, too."

"I don't want you to use me as a toilet," she warned.

That startled a laugh out of him. "Fair enough. What about the rest of it? Do you want to do that again?"

"I really kinda do." She wrinkled her nose at him. "Do you?"

"I really kinda do," he echoed, and leaned down to capture her lips in a soft kiss. "Maybe next time I'll make you come five times."

"Oh, jeez," she muttered, and made him laugh. A sudden thought occurred to her, and she jerked back to frown at him.

"What?"

"That thing you said last night, that you had to fuck my ass because I'd had the dildo in my vagina and it would probably be too loose for you to feel."

His eyes twinkled, clearly amused. "What about it?"

"You know that doesn't actually happen like that, right? The vagina is incredibly elastic, and would return to its normal shape and size within—"

He cut her off with another kiss, lingering over it until she softened against him, then raised his head to wink at her. "I know. But it was hot, wasn't it?"

She choked on a laugh. "That's not the point."

"Baby, it's exactly the point. We'll talk about this some more, all right? And I'll do some research before we play with it again."

"What kind of research?"

He wiggled his fingers. "The internet kind. I don't know anyone personally who does humiliation play. Unless..."

"What?"

"Jack might have some experience," he said, and arched an eyebrow in question. "Are you all right if I talk to him about it?"

She thought of their friend with some alarm. "I don't know if I want you getting play tips from a sadist."

He grinned. "I've gotten plenty of play tips from him."

Her eyes narrowed. "Which ones?"

"You liked all of them," he assured her.

"Hmmm." She narrowed her eyes at him. "Okay, you can talk to him. But I want to know what he says. And we'll talk before we go any further, right?"

"Deal." He leaned his forehead against hers. "You know I love you, Mandy."

She sighed. It always made her go mushy when he called her Mandy. "I know. I love you, too."

He kissed her again. "I'm hungry. Want to go out for lunch?"

"I haven't even had breakfast yet," she protested.

"That's because you slept until almost eleven," he pointed out, and gave her a last, smacking kiss before nudging her off his lap. "If it makes you feel better, we can call it brunch."

"Fine." She headed for the stairs, then paused with her foot on the bottom step to frown at him. "The electric fly swatter was Jack's idea, wasn't it?"

He just grinned and started up the stairs, leaving her to follow, wondering what she'd gotten herself into.

Chapter Four

Two weeks later, James was in the basement re-stocking the bar in anticipation of his guests' arrival. The open space was warm, thanks to excellent insulation and the gas fireplace, and he'd turned on the lights in the game area. The basement ran the length of the house and had two guest bedrooms, each with its own bath, wide French doors that led to a walkout patio, and a half bath under the stairs. They'd renovated it at the end of the summer, outfitting it with soft carpet and recessed lighting, and it made for excellent entertaining space of both the kinky and vanilla varieties. Amanda had held her PR company's holiday party there, and a week later they'd hosted a similar party for all their kinky friends.

Well, not *exactly* similar.

The kinky furniture had been since stored away, so the large sectional sofa and comfortable club chairs in dark leather were grouped around the fireplace, an old trunk serving as a coffee table in the middle, and the other side of the room held the portable bar and gaming area. There was a round table with half a dozen chairs that could be used for poker or board games, a large screen mounted to the wall for video games or movies, and the newest addition sat in the middle of the room.

Amanda had given him the custom pool table for Christmas. The carved walnut table was topped with grey felt and had a cover that would allow them to use it as a solid surface for entertaining. He'd been worried about how they'd get it out of the way if they needed the space for a club party—it was way too heavy to lift—when Amanda had pointed out that it was on wheels for ease of movement.

He could always count on her to pay attention to the details.

He hadn't played a game yet, with being out of town over New Year's and the work he'd had to catch up on since, but he thought he might get one or two in tonight. Only a few people were coming for the monthly Doms & Tops gathering, and though he normally enjoyed the company of all the friends he'd made in the kink scene, he was glad to have a smaller group this time. Jack had texted earlier to let him know that he'd be there, which meant it was a perfect time to pick his brain regarding humiliation play.

"Babe? You down here?" Amanda called.

"Yep," he called back, and set the ice bucket on the bar before turning to watch her cross the room. He smiled. "You look nice."

"Thanks." She gave a little twirl, the calf-length skirt of her dress floating up around her knees as she moved. The dress was deep green, her knee-high boots nearly the same glossy brown as her hair, and her faux fur was draped over her arm.

She looked good, but she rarely dressed up to go to the Subs & Bottoms meeting. "What's the occasion?"

"We're meeting at Charlie's," she told him, naming a popular tapas bar downtown. "Caroline's mom is still visiting, and a lot of the others cried off, so we decided to make a night of it."

"I'm going to have a light crowd, too." He slipped his arms around her waist and bent down for a kiss. "Who's going?"

"Sadie and Rebecca for sure," she replied, stroking her fingers over his jaw, which was clean-shaven now that he was back at work. "A few of the others might meet us there. Oh, and Sam's going. Collette is still out of town, and he had the night off, so he volunteered to be the designated driver."

James nodded his approval. Sam didn't make it to a lot of club events—his job as a hospital nurse kept him busy, and his schedule wasn't always predictable—but he tended to have a calming influence on some of the rowdier members of the group. "Good for Sam. Are you taking a ride service in?"

"No, he's picking us up. Nick's bringing Sadie and Rebecca here with him, so we'll all head out together."

"You've still got two more days of antibiotics," he reminded her, and gave the flirty ends of her hair a tug. "So no more than two drinks."

"Two?" She stared up at him, her lush lips—painted a glossy pink—turned down in a frown. "Doctor Google said alcohol won't interfere with amoxicillin. And I feel fine."

"Three drinks, then," he amended, and tugged her hair again. "You're still a little run down, and I don't want you relapsing."

"Fine," she mumbled.

He kissed her pouting mouth. "Promise me."

She sighed. "I promise, only three drinks."

"Thank you," he said, and kissed her again.

"You're welcome," she said, most of the pout gone, and glanced around the room. "You didn't set up for poker?"

He shook his head. "Only three people are coming, so I thought I'd try to interest them in a mini pool tournament instead."

"That'll be nice." She turned at the sound of the doorbell. "That's probably Nick and the girls."

"Send Nick on down, would you?"

"Sure." She lifted her face for another kiss. "Have fun tonight."

"You, too. Three drinks," he reminded her.

"I remember," she said with a sassy little eye roll, and skipped out of his reach with a laugh.

"You'll pay for that later," he called after her as she crossed the room.

"Counting on it," she called back, and ran up the steps.

He was checking to make sure he had plenty of the flavored seltzer Cade preferred when heavier footsteps sounded on the stairs. Nick walked into the room, a smile of greeting on his face that fell away when he saw the pool table. "Whoa."

James grinned. "Happy New Year."

"Yeah, right." Nick stepped up to the table and laid a reverent hand on the carved wood. "Where did this beauty come from?"

"Christmas gift from Amanda," James replied, and tilted his head toward the bar. "Want a drink?"

"In a minute." Eyes glued to the table, Nick circled it slowly. "Have I ever told you that you have excellent taste in wives?"

James laughed. "Once or twice."

"Well, it bears repeating." Nick lifted his head, a look of awe on his bearded face. "This is fucking awesome."

"I know. I've been so busy since Christmas that I haven't had time for a game."

"You haven't played on it?" Nick stared. "At *all*?"

James shook his head. "I was hoping we could have a mini tournament tonight."

"Hell, yes." Nick glanced around, spotted the rack of cues on the wall, and strode over to choose his weapon. "Who's going to break?"

"Jack and Cade are coming," James said, amused. "You want to maybe wait for them?"

"Hell, no." Nick pulled down a cue. "They're late, I'm not. Let's play pool."

James laughed and crossed to the rack to choose his own cue. "All right. Nine ball, my break. Rack 'em."

They were halfway through the first game when Jack and Cade arrived, and after some debate it was determined that Cade and Jack would play the second game, then the winners would play.

As luck would have it, James lost to Nick and Jack lost to Cade, so Jack cracked the bottle of scotch he'd brought as a belated Christmas gift, and the two men settled in with a drink to watch the winners' match.

"We were sorry you couldn't make it to the club holiday party," James began.

Jack nodded, swirling the amber liquid in his glass before taking a sip. "I'm sorry I missed it. Especially the show."

"The show?"

Jack gestured with his glass, the thick silver ring on his middle finger glinting in the light. "Nick and his new lady love."

"Ah. It was touch and go there for a while, but it all worked out in the end."

"He's got fucking stars in his eyes, so I guess so." Jack grinned as Nick sank his ball. "At least they're not messing up his aim."

They watched Nick sink another ball, then miss on a bank shot and step back from the table with a scowl for Cade to take over.

"How's the liquor supply business going?" James ventured.

"Can't complain." Jack crossed his legs and leaned back in the chair, the picture of relaxed elegance in trim slacks and crisp white shirt. The tattoos peeking out from under the open French cuffs added an edge to the image of the polished urban professional. "People love to drink during the holidays. It's been tough to find time to play, though."

"Are you still seeing Clarice?"

Jack shook his head. "Things fizzled there. She was down to play, but not much else."

James eyed his friend, a little surprised. "That's a problem for you?"

Jack shrugged. "I'm getting a little bored with the submissive shuffle."

That startled a laugh out of James. "Submissive shuffle?"

"You know what I mean. I'm thirty-seven, and it turns out I might like to try an actual relationship."

"You got anybody in mind?"

Jack shook his head. "Not at the moment."

"Want me to ask Amanda if she has any single friends?"

Jack's dark gaze shot to James, genuine alarm on his handsome face. "Fuck, no," he blurted out, his normally low voice rising an octave in panic. "No matchmaking."

James laughed so hard he had to set his drink down. "You should see your face," he managed, laughing harder when Jack scowled.

"Ass," he grumbled, but his lips twitched. "Don't scare me like that."

"Sorry, I couldn't resist." James retrieved his drink and eyed the pool players. Cade and Nick were in the middle of a heated argument about whether or not Cade had prevented the seven ball from rolling into a side pocket, and neither man was paying him or Jack any attention.

"You mind if I pick your brain for a minute on something?" he asked.

Jack eyed him warily. "About what?"

James grinned. "I'm not gathering information for your season on BDSM Bachelor, so relax."

Jack snorted into his drink, then paused, considering. "I bet people would watch that."

"No doubt." James turned in his chair slightly to face the other man more fully. "Amanda and I ran into something new, and I thought you might have some insight."

"On?"

"We sort of stumbled our way into an erotic humiliation scene a few weeks ago."

Both eyebrows shot up. "Seriously?"

James nodded, and briefly described how the scene had played out. "We talked it out the next morning, and several times since. We'd both like to explore it further, but neither of us has done this before. I've done some internet research, but I thought you might have some experience."

"Some." Jack tapped his finger against his glass, the ring clinking dully against the crystal. "I usually prefer to express my sadism in more physical ways, but I've done some erotic humiliation. It can be tricky."

"I know. We're taking it slow," James assured him. "Amanda's been sick this month, too, and I didn't want to take the next step until she was back to full health."

"Smart," Jack murmured, and tapped his glass again. "There are levels to this, right? Humiliation, degradation, dehumanization, objectification."

"I've already been told that human ashtray and/or toilet is off the table."

Jack grinned. "Okay. Well, that still leaves a lot of room to play. If it were me, I'd set up a few scenes to see what works. Keep them low stakes, keep them brief, but get into it and see what shakes out."

"I have a few ideas on that," James began, and laid out the plan he'd come up with.

Jack pursed his lips. "That covers being in public, being on display, dehumanization—I'd keep that one private, by the way."

"Planned on it."

Jack nodded. "A lot of people who are into shame play are working out trauma with it. I don't need details, obviously, but do you know if there's anything like that in Amanda's background?"

"We've talked about it, and she doesn't think so. Not that something couldn't pop up in a scene, of course." James shrugged. "Brains are tricky."

"That they are. What about you?"

James frowned. "Me?"

"Doms have triggers, too," Jack reminded him.

"Good point," James murmured, a little abashed that he hadn't considered the possibility. "I don't believe so, but I'll have to put some thought into it."

"Do that, and it sounds like you're on the right track. Take it slow, keep talking it out. You know the drill."

"Yeah." James reached out and tapped his glass against Jack's. "Thanks."

Jack inclined his head. "Anytime."

"And seriously, if you want some help finding a girlfriend, I'm sure Amanda would be willing to lend a hand."

"Don't make me hurt you," Jack warned, and James laughed.

"Hey," Nick called. "Cade cheats at pool."

Cade smirked. "You're just mad I handle a cue better than you."

"There's a jerk-off joke in there somewhere," James said drily, and pushed to his feet as Nick scowled and Jack laughed. "All right, assholes. It's my table—I'm playing."

"Play the cheater," Nick said, still scowling, and handed his cue to James. "I'm going to go drink with Jack and get some ideas about how to hurt my woman."

"What is this, ask a sadist day?" Jack wondered.

"You're never around lately, so I'm seizing the fucking moment," Nick settled into the chair James had just vacated. "Can I borrow your single tail?"

Jack blinked. "Since when do you know how to use a single tail?"

"I don't. I just want to borrow it to scare Rebecca."

Cade finished racking the balls and straightened. "She have a whip phobia or something?"

"No."

"Then what makes you think she won't call your bluff?"

"Shit," Nick muttered, and turned his scowl on Jack. "Can you teach me to use a single tail?"

"I have to meet this woman," Jack muttered.

James chalked his cue and leaned over the table to line up his shot. "Speaking of Rebecca, does she have any single, kinky friends she can introduce Jack to? He's looking for a girlfriend."

"No shit?" Cade leaned a hip on the table. "You thinking of giving up your subscription to the Masochist of the Month Club?"

Jack glared at James. "I'm taking my scotch back."

James broke, the clatter of balls mingling with his friends' laughter.

Chapter Five

Amanda stepped into the house a week later and sighed with relief. Work had been one headache after another all day, and all she wanted was a glass of wine and twenty minutes of peace and quiet. If James was finished working and could be conscripted into playing foot masseur, she'd be in heaven.

She slipped out of her shoes, wiggling her toes against the cold tile, and with her arches still screaming from being jammed into the three-inch heels, shuffle-walked her way to the closet. Bag and coat put away, she headed immediately for the kitchen and the open bottle of red wine left over from dinner last night.

The fireplace was on, though James wasn't lounging in his usual spot on the sofa. She thought briefly about hunting him up, then rejected the idea in favor of getting off her feet faster. She was pouring a glass when James called her name.

"Mandy?"

"It's me," she called back. "I'm having wine. You want?"

"Go ahead and pour me a glass. I'm wrapping something up, be down in five."

She poured the second glass and took both with her to the living room. She took a healthy sip of hers before setting both on the coffee table and stretching out full length on the sofa. She let her eyes drift closed with a sigh.

Five minutes later she was roused from her light doze by her husband's low chuckle. "Rough day?"

"It sucked," she told him, not bothering to open her eyes. "New clients who think they know everything, multiple meetings, worked through lunch. The car ride home was the first time I sat down since noon."

"Aw," he said, his voice much closer, and she smiled a little as he pressed a soft kiss to her mouth. "Better?"

"Better," she allowed, then forced her smiling lips into a pout. "But my feet really hurt."

"Do they?" he said, amusement creeping into his tone.

She opened her eyes, making sure to flutter her lashes a bit, and put on her best *pretty please* face. "Would you rub them for me, please?"

He grinned down at her. "Wow, I got the big eyes and everything."

"All afternoon on my feet. In high heels. I'll beg if I have to."

He chuckled and moved to the end of the couch. "I won't make you go that far. I like to save the begging for more pleasurable activities."

She smirked and sat up, scooting back to lean against the cushions, and lifted her feet so he could sit down. "Right now, I'll take the foot rub over an orgasm."

"Well, then." He set his wine on the end table and drew her feet into his lap. He skimmed a palm up her arches. "Stockings or pantyhose?"

"Stockings," she said with an anticipatory sigh.

He tapped her big toe. "Let's get them off, so I can do a proper job."

She wiggled her skirt up to expose the top of the thigh-high stockings, and his eyebrows rose. "No garters? I thought you hated the stay-put kind."

She shook her head and reached for the one on her right leg. "Rebecca said she'd had good luck with this brand, so I thought I'd give them a try." She winced as she rolled down the top, the silicone grip strip that made the stocking stay up without garters tugging at her skin. "I still hate them."

She shoved the delicate hose down past her knee, not caring if they tore since she had no intention of ever putting them on again. He peeled it the rest of the way off her leg while she went to work on the left one, rubbing absently at the red marks the bands had left on her thighs.

"Almost looks like rope marks," he commented, setting the stockings aside.

"Almost feels like rope marks." She leaned over to grab her wine from the coffee table, then snuggled into the cushions. "They were too tight."

"Too small?"

She shook her head. "They're the right size. They just have to be tight to stay up. I'm sticking with the kind that need help to stay up from now on."

"Fine with me," he declared, and picked up her right foot and began to rub.

"You just like looking at my ass when I wear garters," she teased.

"Hell, yes." He winked at her, digging his thumbs into her aching arch. "How's this feel?"

"Amazing," she sighed. She sipped her wine while he worked, fighting the desire to just close her eyes and drift off. "Tell me about your day."

He smiled at her knowingly, his fingers continuing to wield their magic. "You can go to sleep if you want."

"I don't want to go to sleep. I feel like we haven't talked in a couple of days. And we haven't had sex since I got sick." She tried another pout. "I miss your dick."

He snorted out a laugh. "I miss your pussy. But you're tired, and we have all weekend to get back on track."

"Really? No projects this weekend?"

He shook his head. "I cleared the decks. How about you? Anything on your plate that needs handling?"

"Nope." She wiggled with glee. "We can stay naked all weekend."

"Funny you should mention that."

She hummed absently as she sipped her wine, then realized he was looking at her with an intensity that made the hair on the back of her neck stand up. "What?"

"Remember what we've been talking about?" He set her right foot down and picked up her left.

"The humiliation play," she remembered with a little jolt.

"I have a plan," he said, and waggled his eyebrows.

She laughed, but there was a little ball of apprehension in her belly. "Weren't you going to talk to Jack?"

"Did that," he told her. "When they were here playing pool."

"Oh."

He chuckled, reading her easily. "You forgot about it, didn't you?"

"I guess I did," she admitted. "I mean, we talked a lot about it, but then I got sick and I've been playing catch-up at work, so it slipped my mind."

"Are you still interested?"

"I think so." She frowned, trying to recall the details of the scene they'd done right after New Year's. She remembered it being hot, and she remembered being forced into multiple orgasms, and she remembered feeling embarrassed that he had watched it all, detached and from afar. "Do I get to hear it?"

He considered that for a moment, his hands continuing to rub. "The general plan," he finally decided. "No details."

She wasn't surprised. He wouldn't spring something wholly unexpected on her, but he did like to keep a trick or two up his sleeve. "Okay."

"Essentially, I've planned out a few scenes to see how we like the various levels of erotic humiliation."

"Levels?"

"I'm sure there's more nuance to this than I'm aware of, but to start we're talking about humiliation, degradation, dehumanization and objectification."

She raised a hand. "Whichever one of those covers the human ashtray and toilet scenarios, I veto."

"I remember." He gave her foot a reassuring pat. "They—and related activities—are off the table. In fact, we'll probably leave degradation out altogether. It feels…"

"Like too much," she finished, and he nodded.

"Especially since we're new at this. I want to start slow."

She let out a slow breath. "Okay, good. So, what's first on the agenda?"

"Dehumanization."

She frowned. "I don't know what that will look like."

"That's okay. I do."

When she shot him an exasperated look, he patted her foot again. "You'll have your safeword, as always. And if you don't like it or it makes you uncomfortable, we stop. But honestly? I think you'll like this."

"You do, huh?" She shook her head, but she was smiling. His eyes were dancing with a combination of humor and anticipation, and his lips were curled in what could only be described as a gleeful grin. She loved that he was never afraid to show enthusiasm, to show her how much he enjoyed exploring kink with her. So many dominants maintained a stern façade all the time, and James was certainly capable of that—that first humiliation scene was an excellent example—but he was never afraid to show his joy.

"I really do. And I *know* I'll like it."

She laughed when he winked again. "Okay, Sir. I'm yours for the weekend."

He lifted her foot to give it a smacking kiss. "That's my girl. Noon tomorrow."

She blinked in surprise. "We're doing an all-day scene?"

"In a manner of speaking. I want you to get a good night's sleep, and in the morning, take a bath. I've got Sadie coming in to give you a massage at ten-thirty."

Amanda's eyebrows shot up. "Seriously?"

"I want you nice and relaxed."

"Before you make me nice and tense?" she guessed drily.

"Nice and anxious. Just a little bit."

"Uh-huh." Some of that anxiety was already trickling in, but she didn't mind. She liked the anticipation, and the sense of unease that came with not knowing exactly what was going to happen. She trusted James. Keeping her safe was his priority, and knowing that meant she could follow his lead into dark corners.

"In the meantime," he went on, "I ordered dinner. It's keeping warm in the oven."

"Oh, excellent." She wiggled her toes in his lap. "Can we eat it here?"

"Sure. But only one more glass of wine. I don't want you dehydrated tomorrow."

"Okay." There were only about two glasses left in the bottle, anyway. "Then after, sex."

"No."

"Huh?"

"No sex." He patted her ankle, then shifted her feet off his lap and pushed to his feet.

"What happened to 'I miss your pussy'?" she wanted to know.

"I do. And I'm going to be getting plenty of it tomorrow." He slipped on a pair of oven mitts and pulled an aluminum tray from the oven.

"Oh, I get it." She twisted around on the couch so she could watch him work. "This is you keeping me horny for whatever shenanigans you have planned."

He plated the pasta and roasted vegetables with a chuckle. "You see right through me."

"I could just take care of business myself, you know," she teased, and fluttered her lashes innocently when he turned on her with an icy gaze.

"Don't even think about it," he warned, and she knew he wasn't kidding. After fourteen years, she could pretty much tell when there was room to wiggle around an order for fun and when disobedience would end very, very badly.

"Fine," she said with a grumpy scowl that was only partly affected. She'd really been looking forward to sex, dammit. "Whatever you've got planned better be worth the wait."

He carried the plates over, his smile sharp as a blade. "You'll see."

Her belly gave another little flutter, and she could tell by the way his eyes gleamed that he knew it. "You're such a pervert."

He put the plates on the coffee table and leaned down to kiss her, hard and quick. "That's why you love me."

"Well, it's one of the reasons," she admitted breathlessly when he lifted his head.

He laughed and handed her a fork, kissed her again, and sat down beside her. "Come on, let's eat. Then you can pick out a movie to fall asleep to."

She snorted out a laugh and ate.

* * * *

She did fall asleep during the movie, but she'd picked *The Fugitive* so James wouldn't mind sitting through it without her, and she woke the next morning to breakfast in bed. James had said he wanted her well fed, and he'd made French toast and bacon to prove it.

Breakfast over, he nudged her to take a long bubble bath, and when she got out, Sadie was already in the bedroom, her portable massage table set up and waiting.

Amanda climbed onto the table. "I can't believe he did all this."

Sadie let out a sigh and draped the sheet over Amanda's lower back, her topknot of ginger hair gleaming in the light of the half-dozen candles flickering around the room. "He's so sweet."

Amanda wiggled into place. "He's softening me up to do horrible things to me. He didn't tell you what he's up to, did he?"

"Of course not. All he told me was he wanted you relaxed and feeling good."

"Figures," Amanda muttered.

"Any injuries or sore spots I need to be aware of?"

"Not really," Amanda said, already relaxing into the table. "I carry my stress in my shoulders, so they're probably in knots."

Sadie laid her hands, slick with warm oil, on Amanda's bare shoulders. "Work making you crazy?"

"Always," Amanda mumbled, grunting a little at the strong press of Sadie's hands. "God, that feels good. You can go a little harder."

"I don't want to tear you up too much," Sadie told her. "This is supposed to be a relaxing massage, not deep tissue torture."

Amanda sighed. "Fine. But I'm coming to see you next week so you can dig in."

"Up to my elbows," Sadie promised with a laugh.

The rhythmic strokes were hypnotic, and Amanda found herself drifting. She roused when Sadie whispered that it was time to turn over, then blissed out again while Sadie worked on her feet, legs, arms and neck.

She blinked back to reality when the music shut off. "Whoa."

"Yeah, you dropped out." Sadie laid a hand on her shoulder, covered now in the light, soft sheet. "Take your time getting up. No fast movements. There's a bottle of water on the dresser. Drink it all. James said to meet him in the basement when you're ready, and he left you a robe on the bed."

"Okay. Give me a second and I'll get up so you can gather up your stuff."

"No rush. When you go down, I'll pack up and get out of your hair."

"I'd invite you to stay for lunch, but I have no idea what he's got planned."

"Whatever it is, I don't think I'm invited," Sadie said with a low laugh. "Take your time, okay? I'll be in the kitchen."

"Thanks," Amanda said again, and pushed herself up to sit on the table as the door shut quietly behind Sadie. She picked up the water and drank deeply, then slipped off the table and balled up the sheet for the hamper. The robe James had left behind was one of his, the soft cashmere one he'd had forever and hardly ever let her wear because he said he had to have one robe she didn't steal. It was thick and soft, wrapping around her like a big, gentle hug. The pale blue color was nearly the shade of James' eyes, and when she buried her nose in the lapels, it smelled like him.

She carried her water with her down the stairs, sipping steadily. She poked her head into the kitchen to let Sadie know she was clear to gather up her things, gave her a quick hug, then continued down to the basement.

James was stretched out on the sectional in a pair of jeans and a cable knit sweater, the fireplace behind him crackling away. His feet were bare. He looked up with a smile. "Hello, love."

"Hi." She leaned down to kiss him, enjoying the scruff of his weekend beard against her skin. "Thanks for the robe."

"It's just a loan," he warned her, and gave her hair a tug.

"Damn," she grumbled, pleased when he chuckled.

"Sit with me for a minute." He tugged her down into his lap. "How do you feel?"

"I feel great." She tipped her head back to beam at him. "Relaxed. Limber. I need to see Sadie more often."

"Not a terrible idea. Are you tired?" He stroked a hand over her hair, her face. "Any lingering symptoms from the tonsillitis?"

She shook her head. "I feel fine, James. Really. All better."

"All right, then. Finish your water and hit the bathroom to take care of any pressing business."

She tipped the bottle back to drain it. "I don't have any pressing business."

"Go anyway," he said, his eyes lit with amusement. "Then meet me back here."

She narrowed her eyes at him, suspicious, but he only smiled. "You're just trying to make me nervous," she said as she eased off his lap.

His smile turned a little wicked at the edges. "I'm not trying to, but it's a nice side benefit."

"Pervert," she accused, trying and failing to suppress the nerves that were beginning to do their jittery dance in her belly.

"Go," he repeated, and gave her butt a smack to enforce the order.

"I'm going, I'm going," she muttered, and hurried over to the powder room tucked under the stairs. Taking care of business didn't take long, and though she was tempted to linger in the bathroom so he'd have to fetch her, she didn't think it would start their day off on the right note. Whatever he'd planned, he'd clearly gone to a great deal of trouble to set it up, and she didn't want to ruin it.

She drew a deep breath, reminded herself that her husband loved her, would never hurt her, and that her safeword always worked, then stepped out of the bathroom.

"All right, Mister Sneaky Dom," she began as she turned the corner, then stopped short when she saw the items laid out on the pool table. She stared at them, her heart thundering in her ears, before shifting her gaze to him. "You're kidding."

Chapter Six

James watched her jaw drop and wondered if he'd made a huge mistake.

He'd laid out the newly purchased gear on the pool table so she could see each piece. The headband with the fluffy, pointed ears, the mittens and booties in the same gray-tipped white fur. He hadn't been able to get a pair of knee pads to match, but they were gray, and they'd keep her knees from getting rug-burned and sore. Then there was the collar, the leash, and lastly, the butt plug decorated with a fluffy white tail.

"You're kidding," she finally said, and though her voice held shock, he was relieved there was no revulsion or anger.

He kept his own voice steady and calm. "Nope. Dehumanization day is puppy play day."

"Puppy play." She swallowed, her eyes on the array of gear.

"Do you hate the idea?"

"No," she said slowly. "I don't hate it. It's like…toast."

"Toast?"

"Yeah. Nobody hates toast, nobody loves toast. It's just…toast."

He stifled a laugh. "You're not saying no, then."

"I'm not saying no." She lifted her confused gaze to his. "I just don't understand what this is supposed to do."

"It's supposed to allow us to find out if dehumanization is something you enjoy." He held up the ears, smothering a laugh when her eyes followed them, her throat bobbing as she swallowed.

"Okay." She wiped her palms on the robe, her eyes still locked on the ears. "What are the rules?"

"Simple," he said, and reached out to slip the headband over her dark cap of hair. "You're a puppy. If a puppy would do it, you can do it. If a puppy wouldn't do it, neither can you."

Her eyes were like saucers. "What about my safeword?"

"For yellow, it'll be the same as when you're gagged, with a little puppy twist. Three barks, or," he said, his eyes twinkling at her, "you pound your paw three times."

"Funny," she muttered, but her cheeks were flushed, and her pulse fluttered at the base of her throat. "And for red?"

"For red, you can break character and just say red."

She nodded. "For how long?"

He reached for the belt on her robe, moving slowly to give her plenty of time to stop him, and slipped the knot free. "All day."

"All *day*?" she squeaked and didn't even twitch when the robe pooled on the floor.

He stroked his hands down her arms to take her hands. "We're at home, just the two of us." He'd wanted low stakes, and low pressure. "You don't have to worry about anything this afternoon except accessing your inner puppy."

"My inner puppy?" She sputtered, the ears on her head bouncing with the bob of her head. "I'm going to feel ridiculous, James."

"If you do, you do." He squeezed her hands, then released them and turned back to the table. "It's just another role play, after all. Right?"

"Right." She stared at the mittens he held out. "What're those?"

"Paws," he said with a grin. "Hold out your hands."

She giggled, making the ears bounce again, but she held out her hands and let him fit the mits on. They were soft, lined with flannel to keep her hands warm and safe, with Velcro straps at the wrist to hold them in place. He'd seen plenty of options online with buckles or even locks, but figured for this scene the Velcro was a better option. He had no idea how she'd react to this, and wanted to be able to get her out of them quickly if he had to.

"How do they feel?"

She lifted her hands, the fur rippling as she flexed her fingers inside the mitts. She turned them around to look at their palms, giggling again when she saw the small patches of pink vinyl that mimicked the pads of a dog's paw.

"They think of everything, don't they?" She flexed her hands at the wrists. "They feel good."

"Not too snug?"

"Not at all," she said, still looking at her hands with something akin to awe.

"Good. If that changes, let me know." He turned back to the table to pick up the kneepads and booties and knelt in front of her. "Lift your right foot."

She frowned but complied, watching him pull the wide cuffed elastic of the kneepad up around her knee. "Why do I need kneepads?"

He picked up the other pad and tapped the top of her left foot. "Puppies don't walk on two feet, darling."

He glanced up to find her eyes even wider and her mouth hanging open. "You're going to make me *crawl*?"

He choked back a laugh as he tugged the second pad into place, then picked up the booties. "Right foot again," he ordered, and quickly strapped them in place.

He rose to his feet. "Comfortable?"

She lifted one foot, then the other, almost dancing in place. "They just feel like fuzzy socks."

"Excellent." He turned and picked up the bright pink collar. It was lined with white faux fur that stuck out a few inches on either side of the shiny vinyl and would make her neck look as though it was circled in the same fur decorating her ears and paws. It had *Mandy* painted on it in white flowing script, and a little silver bell.

He buckled it on carefully, slipping a finger underneath to make sure it wasn't too tight, then stepped back to judge the effect. "You look adorable."

"Really?" she asked. Her eyes held a kind of shy delight, and her cheeks glowed a fetching pink.

"Absolutely adorable," he assured her, and turned to pick up the butt plug. "One more thing."

"Oh." The collar moved when she swallowed. "Okay."

She started to lean over the pool table, stopping when he said "No."

She glanced up at him in question. "Sir?"

He pointed at the floor. "Down, girl."

Her cheeks went instantly red, but she stepped back from the table and sank gracefully to her knees, then forward onto her hands. Her breasts swayed as she settled into place, her head dipping down and her ears tipping forward, her gaze fixed on the floor.

He crouched down in front of her. "Eyes on me," he said sternly, and her head came up immediately. Her eyes were soft, vulnerable now, but the trust in their dark brown depths was absolute.

"Good girl," he said softly, and stroked his hand over her face. Her lashes fell, shielding her eyes, but she leaned her cheek into his hand, nuzzling the palm. "Good girl," he said again, his fingers moving to grip her chin.

He held up the plug in his other hand, turning it so the attached tail flipped in the air. He waited a beat, wanting to be sure she saw it, before he spoke again. "When this goes in, we're in scene. You're my sweet puppy, Mandy, and we're just hanging out on a Saturday afternoon."

He gave her chin a gentle pinch. "Any questions?"

"No," she whispered.

The tremble in her voice was barely audible, but to him, it was like a sounding gong. He used his grip on her chin to lift it, just a bit, so he could look her in the eye. "I love you, Amanda."

Her breath came out on a sigh, and he saw her answer in her eyes before the words left her mouth. "I love you, too."

He kissed her, pouring every bit of the love and pride he felt for her into it. Then he rose to his feet and circled her kneeling form until he stood behind her.

He eyed the plug in his hand thoughtfully. The tail attached to the plug via a small clip, so he tugged it off and set it aside before pulling the bottle of lubricant out of his pocket. He crouched, stroking a hand over the curve of her ass, and tipped the bottle to allow some of the thick liquid to drip onto the pink pucker of her exposed anus.

She jerked when it hit her skin with a little squeak of shock. He knew she probably hadn't intended it to be, but it was nearly a yip, and charmingly puppy-like.

"Easy, Mandy," he murmured. He patted her hip reassuringly as more lubricant dripped from the bottle, then shifted it to coat the plug. He'd chosen a silicone plug with gentle ribbing to help it stay in better, in a smaller size than he normally would, since she'd be wearing it for much longer than usual. The lube he'd chosen was thick and formulated especially for anal play. He might have to reapply it once or twice during the day, but it should keep her relatively comfortable.

He made sure the plug was slickly coated, then tucked the bottle away and set a hand on her tailbone. "Stay," he ordered, and pressed the tip of the plug to her anus.

She jerked, an instinctive reaction to both the cool plug and the sudden pressure. He raised his hand and delivered a short, hard slap to one cheek. "I said stay," he reminded her sternly, and slowly, steadily, pushed the plug home.

She accepted it with relative ease, the ring of muscle stretching to accommodate the wider middle before clamping down on the narrow neck and drawing it firmly into place. "What a good girl you are," he murmured, "taking that in your pretty little hole so beautifully."

A shiver raced over her skin—whether from the plug settling into place or the words, he wasn't sure. He wiggled the base a bit, making sure it was well seated, then slid his fingers down to skim them over her soft, pretty pussy.

She was wet, and though he knew some of it was the lube that had dripped down from her anus, when he slipped his fingers forward and found her clit already firm and engorged, he grinned. It wasn't *all* the lube.

"Aren't you an eager girl," he marveled, and pleased himself by giving her clit a soft flick.

She jerked, her high whine mixing with the jangle of the bell, and he chuckled.

"Don't worry, pet. We'll get to that." He pulled his fingers free, ignoring both her disappointed wiggle and his own impatience. He pulled a cloth from his back pocket and wiped his hands clean, then picked up her tail and attached it to the plug with a soft click.

"There." He rose to his feet, surprised at how aroused he was. When her butt gave a little twitch and made the tail swish, he laughed, delighted. "What a pretty puppy I have."

He grabbed the leash off the pool table and circled around so he stood in front of her once again. He bent down to clip the leash to the D ring in her collar, frowning when she flinched at the clank of metal on metal.

He gave the leash a small tug. "Look at me, Mandy girl," he said, and she looked up. Her cheeks were flushed, her eyes bright. She was breathing hard but struggling to hide it, her lips parted as she panted.

"Take a breath, girl," he told her, pleased when she immediately complied. He ignored the way her breasts swayed enticingly with the movement, concentrating instead on her eyes, and the anxiety lurking in their soft depths. "Good girl. We're just having fun, okay? There's no pressure, no expectations. It's just a quiet Saturday at home."

She sucked in another breath, blowing it carefully out, and nodded.

"Good girl," he murmured again. "Remember, yellow is three yips or thumps of your paw, and use your voice for red."

She nodded again, one ear flopping forward with the action, and he smiled. "Okay. Let's go upstairs and get some lunch."

He let the grin come when her eyes went wide and gave the leash a gentle tug. He began slowly walking toward the stairs, and she scrambled to crawl along behind him.

* * * *

While James made lunch at the kitchen island, Amanda sat on her haunches at his feet, her mitten-covered hands on the floor in front of her, and tried to wrap her brain around her current predicament.

She wasn't sure how she felt about being a dog, quite frankly, and though the gear was comfortable, it felt strange to be wearing it. The headband slid over her hair every time she moved, and the ears were heavy enough to flop around without pulling it off her head. If she turned her head sharply, she could catch their tufted white tips out of the corners of her eyes. The paws were super soft and felt the most familiar, and if she didn't think about it, she could almost pretend she had mittens on her hands and socks on her feet. But every time she glanced down, she was reminded that these were dog paws.

She picked up a hand—paw—and turned it over to see the circles of pink vinyl stitched into the fur. She wondered idly if she stepped in mud, then onto the floor, if she'd leave a paw print behind.

She set her hand—dammit, *paw*—back on the floor and glanced up at James. He was engrossed in whatever he was making and paying her no attention, so she went back to her mental inventory.

The plug felt familiar as well. She particularly enjoyed anal play, and it wasn't rare for her to wear a plug for a scene or even a day around the house, if James was in a tormenting mood. She rose from her haunches onto all fours and wiggled her butt experimentally. She could feel the plug inside her, shifting and rubbing and activating all those nerves that seemed to be wired directly to her clit. None of that was new, but the tail swishing against her buttocks and the backs of her thighs was.

She wiggled again, concentrating on the sensation of the tail against her skin. The fur was baby soft, and the tail curled down a bit so it brushed against the lower curves of her buttocks and her upper thighs. It felt weird, she decided, and it tickled a bit. But it wasn't uncomfortable, and it wasn't diminishing her enjoyment of the plug at all. In fact, just the opposite.

God, she was so turned on.

She turned to look over her shoulder, and the bell on her collar jingled musically with the movement. She caught a glimpse of white fur at the base of the tail, where it clipped onto the plug—she'd have to take a look at that when this was all over, to see how it all went together—but the rest of the tail was hidden from view. She gave her hips a hard side-to-side shake this time, wanting to see the tail swish, and grinned when it swung into view.

God, this is weird. And hot. Why is this so hot?

James's soft laugh had her swinging back around to face him, the collar once again jingling musically. He was looking at her, his eyes amused, his mouth curled in a soft smile. "Somebody likes her tail," he said mildly, and she looked down as her cheeks heated.

She did like her tail, she realized, and she had no idea how to feel about that.

He laughed again, sent her a wink, and went back to his lunch preparations.

She waited a beat, then sat back on her haunches. He'd pulled a package of deli meat out of the refrigerator, so she was pretty sure he was making a sandwich. But it was slightly annoying that her position at his feet didn't allow her to see exactly what he was doing. It was even more annoying that he was paying her no more attention than he would, well, a dog.

She licked her lips and though over her options. She wasn't allowed to speak unless she needed to safeword, and being annoyed certainly didn't warrant that. She could only use puppy behavior to get his attention, so even though she felt like an idiot, she lifted a paw and patted his knee.

He spared her a sharp glance. "No, Mandy," he said firmly, and turned back to his sandwich.

Before she could reason it through, she did it again, hard enough to make her collar bell ring loudly and her breasts sway.

"I said no," he said, his gaze like steel. "If you're going to be a bad puppy, I'll have to put you in your crate while I eat my lunch."

A crate? *Oh, hell no.* She had no idea if that threat was an idle one or not—she'd seen no evidence of a crate downstairs, and she knew there wasn't one in their bedroom, but that didn't mean he hadn't managed to squirrel one away somewhere just in case she decided to test him. Deciding not to risk it, she let out a soft whine but subsided, easing back to sit more firmly on her heels. The action made the plug inside her shift again, and this time her whine had nothing to do with being scolded.

His eyes danced with wicked delight. "Slutty puppy," he chided gently, and while she blinked in surprise, he picked up a plate and a small bowl. "Come on, let's go to the dining room."

She shifted forward onto all fours and began to crawl after him, her breath coming in shallow pants. She was almost painfully aware of the heavy sway of her breasts beneath her as she moved, the nipples peaked and swollen, of the slick slide of her thighs. She was turned on, and it was confusing the hell out of her.

Her thoughts drew to a halt with a jerk when she accidentally planted a hand on the trailing leash, letting out a startled *oof* and nearly falling on her face. She swiped at the thin length of pink vinyl, trying to pick it up, but the thick mitten made her fingers useless. She pushed it to the side, but when she tried to move forward it slid right back into her path.

She frowned at it for a second, then leaned down and picked it up in her teeth. She had to tilt her head back and clamp her jaw to keep it from slithering free, and she saw James waiting patiently, an indulgent smile on his face as he watched.

"Clever girl," he said, his voice full of pride, and she flushed with pleasure, her whole body going warm.

He turned and walked through the doorway into the dining room and she followed, moving carefully so she wouldn't slip on the hardwoods. The dog paw pad mittens with the added texture kept her from slipping too much, but her knee pads were slick and kept wanting to slide around. By the time she'd made it into the room, he was already seated at his customary place at the head of the long table, the plate in front of him and the bowl set off to the side.

She stopped beside his chair and eased back on her haunches, her mouth watering when she got a look at the thick sandwich on his plate. She could smell the sourdough bread he'd used, see the thick slices of cheese and roast beef. He picked it up and brought it to his mouth for a big bite, and a whine came out before she could stop it.

He glanced down at her as he chewed, his eyes bright with humor. He swallowed and said, "Hungry, Mandy girl?" in a low, rumbling voice that didn't make her think of food at all, and suddenly she was squirming for a completely different reason.

His gaze sharpened, pure lust blazing in his eyes, and for a moment she thought he would say to hell with the scene and fuck her right there on the dining room floor. But then her stomach growled, and though the lust didn't fade, he picked up the bowl.

His smile was wicked. "You're going to have to drop the leash if you want to eat," he told her, and she realized with a start that she was still holding the leash in her mouth.

She bent her head to drop it on the floor, wincing a little when it hit the wood with a wet slap, and a thin trickle of drool dropped from her mouth to land on her breast. Her cheeks flamed with embarrassment, and she lifted a hand to swipe at the wet streak.

His sharp "No!" had her freezing in place.

His hand closed over hers and pushed it back down, then gently cupped her chin and forced it up. His eyes were still bright with lust and humor, but under there was a kind of understanding that inexplicably made her eyes prick with tears.

"Puppies drool," he said calmly, rubbing his thumb over the streak of spittle on her chin, then dropped his hand to her breast. Her breath clogged in her throat as his thumb stroked over the wetness there, rubbing slowly back and forth until her skin was dry.

"There we go," he murmured, and squeezed her breast gently. "All better."

She eyed her breast when he removed his hand, the skin dry and the nipple tight and flushed. When she looked back up at him, the understanding smile had been replaced with a knowing smirk that made embarrassment pour through her. She fought the need to squirm, knowing it didn't matter because he could see it anyway. The embarrassment, the bright flush of shame…and the flood of arousal that followed.

"Now," he said briskly, and picked up the bowl. "Puppies need food. If you eat your lunch like a good girl, you can have a treat after."

She winced a little, bracing herself for him to put the bowl on the floor, wondering how she'd manage that. Then he plucked a piece of roast beef from the bowl and held it out for her.

"Go ahead," he encouraged when she hesitated, and she leaned forward. "But no nipping."

She hesitated, her mouth inches from his fingers. She hadn't even thought of nipping until he'd mentioned it, and suddenly she could see the possibilities for fun in this game. But it wouldn't do to disobey a direct order, at least not this soon. So she took the food from his fingers, keeping her mouth soft, and beamed at him innocently.

He smiled back, clearly not believing it for a minute. "Good girl," he said with a laugh, and held out another piece of roast beef.

Lunch passed quickly, with James alternating feeding her and himself. She followed him into the kitchen, her leash once again clamped between her teeth—this time placed there by James because he'd said it was cute—then into the living room after he'd dealt with the dishes. He sat on the sofa in his usual corner and picked up the book on the end table, then patted the cushion next to him. "Up."

Relieved, she crawled forward and up onto the cushion beside him. He reached up to ease the leash out of her mouth, unclipping and setting it aside. "There we go, that's better. What a pretty girl you are."

She preened a little under the praise, tilting her head into his hand as he stroked over her hair. His hand continued down, trailing down the fuzzy fur and collar covering her neck to her breasts. She was still on all fours, so they dangled down, and she had a brief spurt of anxiety about how they must look. Normally she didn't even think about being naked in front of James—he loved her, and he loved her body, even on the days when she didn't. But now, every worry she had about the effects of gravity and age came rushing to the fore.

"Look at these," he murmured, and her face heated. He lifted one breast in his hand, holding its weight while rubbed her hardening nipple with his thumb, his touch firm, before switching to the other. He stroked them, his touch idle and soft, watching her face all the while.

"My girl is so pretty." He smiled when her blush deepened, then slipped his hand lower to cup the curve of her belly.

She squirmed, uncomfortable. Her belly had gotten softer with age, too, and it sagged in this position. She started to turn, instinct pushing at her to get his hand away from that place she loved least of all. She jolted in shock when he slapped her breast.

"Stop moving," he said, and moved his hand back to her belly. "I own you, Mandy girl," he told her, his gaze holding hers firmly. He stroked his fingers over the soft flesh, his calloused fingertips scraping lightly over her skin. "You're mine, every part of you, and I'll touch you wherever I like. Isn't that right?"

She nodded slightly, feeling the ears on the top of her head bob, and had to swallow hard against the lump in her throat.

"That's right, good girl." He shifted his hand to her hip and gave her a little pat. "Lie down, now. Put your head on my leg."

She turned awkwardly, lowering herself onto her side then rolling half onto her back, twisting at the waist and tucking her legs up. She looked up at him to find him smiling, heat simmering in his gaze.

"You really are adorable," he murmured, and stroked down her torso so his hand lay solid and heavy on her belly once again. "I'm going to rub your belly while I read, Mandy girl. Would you like that?"

Her face flooded with increased heat, but she nodded anyway. His hand felt wonderful on her skin, and the embarrassment was already fading. But he shook his head.

"If you want me to pet your belly, you have to tell me."

She frowned, tilting her head. Tell him? She wasn't allowed to talk.

His eyebrow quirked up, his lips curling into a smile. "You can bark, can't you? Speak, Mandy girl."

Oh my god. Her cheeks felt so hot they might as well be on fire, but his eyebrow only rose higher, intensifying his *I'm waiting* look. She had to swallow twice, but finally she managed to force a faint yip out of her throat.

"Good girl," he praised, and gave her abdomen a long stroke with pride shining in his eyes. "That's my good girl."

Her breath shuddered out with a sigh when he turned his attention to the book in his lap and continued to stroke her. The embarrassment had faded, but the heat was growing.

James kept his touch firm, his strokes steady and even. He turned the page on his book with his free hand, though he hadn't read a word. All his attention was on his wife. She'd been shivering when she'd first lain down, little jerks and trembles as she struggled to get comfortable. She'd finally stretched her legs out a bit, though he'd seen her wince, and he made a note to keep her off her knees for a while. She'd been having some stiffness in the joints recently, and that had been his biggest concern with this whole setup. Well, his biggest physical concern. There were a whole host of psychological concerns clamoring for his attention.

The anxiety that had washed over her when she'd first seen the equipment had mostly faded during lunch. The simple task of eating had calmed her down, allowed her to relax and settle. She'd tensed up again when she'd climbed onto the couch, but most of that had been uncertainty. Moving around on all fours wasn't something she was used to. Even if she was in that position in bed—which she often was—it was usually stationary, and temporary. This was all day, moving through familiar spaces in an unfamiliar way, and her body was tense and awkward as she figured it out.

It was, in a word, adorable.

He frowned slightly and turned another page. Though the logistics of climbing onto the sofa and lying down in puppy mode had given her some anxiety, she hadn't reacted badly until he'd begun to pet her. His stroke on her head hadn't elicited any reaction but delight—she'd pushed her face into his hand readily, like a puppy wanting pets, her face settling into soft, contented lines. But when he'd slid his hand down to her breasts, she'd stiffened. And when he'd continued down her torso, something akin to alarm had sparked along with shame in her eyes.

He thought he knew what that was about, though he made a mental note to bring it up during their post-scene discussion. And he was kicking himself a little, because he hadn't thought of this. Amanda was a curvy woman, and normally she was comfortable in her skin, so he tended to forget that even a woman as confident and secure as his wife was still vulnerable to the ridiculous standards society held women to when it came to their bodies.

It pissed him off, frankly, but he put the irritation aside. She was calm now under the firm strokes of his hand, and had even started to purr. *Maybe we should've gone for kitty play,* he thought with a spurt of amusement, and increased the pressure of his hand.

She wiggled, and, out of the corner of his eye, he saw her stretch slightly. She was definitely calming down, and nearly ready for the next step. Puppies liked to play, and he'd thought long and hard about how he'd like to play with his puppy.

There was the obvious choice, he thought, and shifted to ease the pinch of his jeans around his crotch. He'd been half hard since he'd slipped the ears over her head and petting her wasn't helping his erection go away. He was a little stunned at how much he was looking forward to fucking her like this. Pet play had never been on the list of things he was curious about, but it was proving to be delightfully arousing. The power differential was so explicit that when he thought about it, it made perfect sense that he was so affected.

The D/s arrangement he had with Amanda was simple. In matters of sex, of play, he was in charge, and in everything else, they were equals. He loved that she was strong, and smart, and so eminently capable of handling almost anything that came her way. It was one of the things that had attracted him to her at the beginning. Confidence and strength were two of his major turn ons, and his wife had them in spades.

Which made it all the more delicious, and humbling, when that strong, confident woman handed all that power over to him.

Desire flooded through him, and he took a deep, steadying breath. He had a plan, and he needed to stick to it. This was an experiment and getting his dick wet wasn't the point of it.

Well, it was sort of the point, he mentally amended, but it was going to have to wait.

So far, she didn't seem to be having a great deal of trouble with being a puppy. She'd been embarrassed to crawl, but that had soon faded. She'd been embarrassed to have him touch her, but he thought that was more due to body anxiety than anything else. He thought of his plan for when she inevitably had to use the bathroom. He was certain the humiliation they were looking for would come up then, and he wondered how she'd react to it. He'd even considered creating a rule that would allow her to step out of the scene for those moments, but after talking it out with Jack, had decided not to. The entire point of the experiment was to see how she felt about those moments, to find out if they turned her on, and he was doing neither of them any favors if he allowed them to sidestep.

But he figured it was fifty-fifty odds that she'd safeword out of it.

Right now, though, she was calm and relaxed as he continued to stroke idly. He glanced discreetly at the clock over the mantel—they'd been sitting there for fifteen minutes or so, and Amanda was never patient when she was aroused. She'd been aroused downstairs, her clit swollen, her pupils dilated. That arousal might have faded since, and though he was tempted to slip his hand lower and check, he held off. If she was still worked up, it wouldn't take long for her to begin getting impatient. If she wasn't, he'd move on to the next part of the plan and get her worked up.

He grinned to himself and turned another page. Either way, it would be soon. *Thank God.*

Chapter Seven

Amanda resisted the urge to wiggle and wondered if this was all they were going to do.

It was nice, of course. She was warm and relaxed, lying on the couch with her head on James' lap with his big hand sliding up and down her torso in smooth, firm strokes. He was petting her, and after she'd got past the momentary *what the fuck* mental reaction, she'd found she liked it. A lot. Honestly, if he kept it up, she'd probably fall asleep.

Which was fine. Really. It had been an exhausting week, and a nap sounded great. Except there was a butt plug in her butt—*attached to a tail, for God's sake*—and she'd thought they were going to *do* stuff. Kinky stuff. Not...eat lunch and lie on the couch.

She didn't know anything about puppy play, or how people normally did it. When they'd first started exploring the world of kink, she'd filled out a yes/no/maybe list to gauge where her interests lay.

James had done the same, and since they'd both marked pet play as a 'no', it had never come up.

She wanted to find her phone and google it, but while she didn't know much about how this kind of play worked, she was fairly certain doing an internet search would not be considered acceptable puppy behavior.

James idly turned the page of his book, seemingly content to just sit there, and she stifled a sigh. She knew better, of course. Her husband had a devious and perverted mind, God love him, and she'd bet her retirement fund he had plans beyond snuggling and reading. But she was getting impatient, and she wasn't sure how long she could keep being a good girl.

She thought of Sadie and stifled a giggle. Had she known what was in store for her today, she'd have picked Sadie's brain on the best ways to get a Dom's attention. Sadie was well known in their little circle for being a brat, and she reveled in her status. Amanda, on the other hand, could only really let the bad girl inside her loose if that was part of the role play, which was probably why their kink included a fair bit of it.

Then realization hit. *That's all this is, really.* It was role play, pure and simple, and she was wasting it.

She thought for a minute, trying to figure the best way forward, then gave a mental shrug. *Puppies like to play, right?* So, she'd start there.

His arm was stretched out to stroke down her torso, his biceps and elbow almost directly above her face. Without giving herself time to think it through, she reached up with her two mittened hands—*paws*, she corrected herself, *they're paws*—and batted at his arm.

He shook his arm lightly and said, "No", his voice calm, almost absent, and flipped another page in his book.

Puppies don't know what 'no' means, she reminded herself with a soundless giggle, and did it again.

"Mandy, no," he said again, this time a bit more firmly. But there was a laugh lurking just under the words, and she knew he didn't mean it. And if she was wrong, well, he'd have to punish her, and at least they'd be doing *something*.

She reached up again, and, remembering something she'd seen her dad's various dogs do over the years, wrapped her paws around his arm and tried to pull it down.

He shook free easily and delivered a light slap to her belly in admonishment. "No, puppy. It's not play time yet. Let me finish my book first."

Play time? She managed to turn her giggle into an appropriately canine-sounding whine and wiggled a little. He'd stopped stroking, his palm heavy on her belly and his arm extended over her head. If he'd *really* wanted her to stop, she reasoned, he'd have removed his arm altogether. She wiggled again, shifting so she was fully on her back, and reached up. This time she wrapped her paws around his arm, and, using it to pull herself up, opened her mouth and nipped at his elbow.

"Ouch!"

He jerked, she guessed more in surprise than in actual pain. She hadn't bitten him *that* hard, but he slapped her belly again.

"Mandy, I said no," he told her, his voice slightly harder now. But he put his book aside and looked down at her, an exasperated expression on his face that couldn't quite hide the delight.

She growled low in her throat, surprising herself by adding an enthusiastic yip at the end, and tried to bite his arm again.

"Oh, you want to play?" he asked, delight in his voice. He covered her face with his free hand, gently pushing her away and ruffling her hair at the same time. "Is that it? Does Mandy want to play?"

She yipped again, the noise slipping from her throat easily, and tried to drag his arm down so she could pretend to gnaw on it.

He laughed and turned to rub both hands over her. "Oh, Mandy wants to wrestle, doesn't she? Is that what she wants?"

She blinked in surprise. They often played games where she got to be bratty and sarcastic and defiant, but they never wrestled, or did anything where she was allowed to bite or scratch or try to best him physically. She never would, anyway. She was strong, and running kept her in reasonably good shape, but he was stronger, and his exercise of choice was martial arts. Unless he was sick or hurt, she wasn't going to beat him in hand-to-hand. But now she'd get to try, and it sounded *glorious.*

She nodded, a series of excited yips and growls coming out of her mouth while she tried to hold on to his arm and bite him. Gently, because she didn't want to hurt him, and because she didn't want the playful tone of the moment to change.

So she used her teeth and her tongue as a puppy would, with nibbling little bites and soft licks, loving the way he laughed and shoved at her with his hands.

"All right, all right. Hold on a minute, Mandy. Mandy, stop."

She froze, the steel in his voice penetrating her happy-puppy haze, and looked up at him.

He gave her head a scrubbing pat. "Good girl. Stay there while I move the table, all right? Can you stay?"

She nodded and released his arm. She stayed where she was, sprawled on the sofa in what she was sure was a completely inelegant display, arms and legs akimbo and breathing hard, but she didn't care. She wasn't Amanda right now, public relations professional and wife. She was Mandy, a happy puppy who didn't concern herself with looking young or beautiful or sexy. Mandy just had fun.

James stood and pushed the coffee table out of the way, then the chairs that sat on the other side, creating a large space on the rug in front of the couch. He sat on his haunches and turned to her with a smile. "Come on, Mandy, come down."

Amanda scrambled to obey, falling to her hands and knees on the floor and hurrying to sit in front of him. "Good girl," he crooned, lifting both hands to stroke over her face. He reached up into her hair and adjusted her headband. No doubt it had gotten knocked askew while they were on the couch, and she giggled.

He grinned down at her. "I like seeing my Mandy-girl happy," he told her, and gave her hair a last pat. "You want to play, Mandy-girl? Do you?"

She nodded and barked, a high-pitched sound that made him laugh.

"All right, we'll play," he said, and with a gentle hand on her shoulder, shoved her over.

She yipped in surprise—it was a little weird how she'd fallen right into those puppy sounds—and scrambled back on to her hands and knees. She lowered her chest to the floor and pushed her butt high in the air in the best approximation of a dog's play bow that she could manage, gave a wiggle and growled.

His laugh rang out, a joyful sound that was cut off abruptly when she pounced on him.

They rolled across the rug, his laughter mixing with her yips and growls and barks. He shoved her with gentle hands, and she battered at him with her paws and did her best to keep her nips light.

"Oh, such a happy puppy," he exclaimed as he rolled her to her back. She struggled to turn, to push up onto all fours so she could pounce again, but this time he kept her pinned, and his hands, only moments before pushing and patting, curved over her breasts.

She stilled at the contact, a startled yip slipping from her throat. Her skin was damp from the tussle, warm and soft, and his hands were hard. He plucked at her nipples, the restraint he'd shown during their wrestling match gone, and this time the yip she let out was higher.

He laughed, and this time his delight had a darker, sharper edge. "That's my girl," he murmured. "You've been a good girl, Mandy. Good girls get rewarded, don't they?"

She could only pant in response. The desire she'd felt when he'd pushed the plug into her ass over an hour ago came roaring back, pumping through her like a drug. Her nipples were hard under his fingers, her breasts swelling with arousal and need. Her pussy gave a hard pulse and her hips jerked in reaction, the movement making the plug shift inside her, and her pussy clamped down again in response.

"Oh, my girl wants a reward, doesn't she?" James purred, and slid his hand away from her breasts, down the damp skin of her belly, to tangle in her pubic hair.

He tugged lightly, pulling up so the skin around her clit tightened, and her hips rolled in response. "Yes, she does."

He tugged her pubic hair again, then let it go. She held her breath, waiting for the touch of his hand on her pussy. She gave a startled yip of surprise when instead, he gripped her hip and flipped her over onto her belly.

"Ass in the air, Mandy-girl," he said, and she complied, pushing her knees under her hips so her butt stuck up high. She started to push her torso up as well, but a firm tap on her butt made her freeze. "No, keep your little paws right where they are," he said, so she stayed put, her butt high and her cheek pressed to the rug, waiting for whatever he had planned next.

"There we go," he said, his voice ripe with satisfaction. "There's that pretty tail I wanted to see."

She blushed, her cheeks hot as she realized what she must look like. She could feel the tail against the lower curves of her buttocks and her upper thighs. She wiggled a little, an instinctive reaction to the tickling caress, and the soft fur brushed against her exposed labia.

He tsked under his breath. "Look what you've done, Mandy-girl," he admonished lightly, and she felt him lift the tail out of the way. "You've gotten your tail all wet."

She pushed her face into the rug, cheeks flaming, when he lifted the tail. The plug seated firmly in her backside moved slightly, and the sudden stimulation made her pussy clench. She pictured what he must be seeing, her upturned ass speared by the plug, the tail firmly attached, and below, her embarrassingly wet pussy.

The thought made her clench down again, and she couldn't hold back the moan.

"That's my girl," he said softly. There was another slight tug on the plug, then she felt the tail brush against her lower back. He'd turned it, she realized, and in doing so exposed everything.

It was nothing he hadn't seen before, she reminded herself. They'd had sex in this position hundreds of times over the years, and that didn't even factor in all the times she'd been bent over the bed, or a bench, or his lap for a spanking. So why did this time feel so different?

Maybe it was that the power differential was so acute. Puppies were literally owned, and even though it was just another role, it made a difference. She'd never wanted to be a slave, and James had never asked it of her, but if this was the way it felt she could understand the appeal. She felt completely controlled in a way she never did when they were just James and Amanda. And in a way, completely free. She didn't have to worry about anything except being what she was in that moment—a puppy who just wanted her owner to play with her.

And oh, she did. Her pussy felt swollen, her clit engorged. Her inner lips would be bright pink, plumped with blood and flowering open to reveal the tender opening behind. *Not opening*, she thought, *hole.* Her pretty little hole would be nearly visible, wet and begging for something to fill it.

Just like last night, that one word sent her head spinning. Her pussy pulsed—*hard*—clenching on nothing even as her anus clamped down on the invading plug, and both sensations made her moan again.

"Oh, yes," James said softly. "Just look at that pretty little hole."

She wanted so badly to speak, to beg him to fill her, but contented herself with a high whine. *Look at it,* she thought wildly, pushing her hips even higher so he could see clearly how much she wanted, needed, to be fucked. *Look at my pretty, greedy hole. I need you, need your cock. Please, fuck me.*

"You want to be fucked, Mandy-girl?" he said. She jerked, her breath whining out as he circled that tender, slick opening with one rough fingertip. She tried to push her hips back even farther, wanting nothing more than to impale herself on that probing finger, and jerked when he slapped her ass. "Keep still," he warned her, "or you won't get to play."

She bit her tongue against the pleas that wanted to spill out and forced her body into stillness. "That's my good girl," he said, and rewarded her with another light stroke over her cunt. "Oh, you do want to play. Why, this pussy is so wet, so eager, it's practically sucking my finger right in."

She held perfectly still as he slid his fingertip inside her, but she couldn't help the way her pussy clamped down. His rich chuckle made her cheeks flush hotter. "Sucking it right in," he said again, his amusement plain, and slid in just a fraction deeper.

She was concentrating so hard on not moving that she didn't feel him shift, then suddenly his voice was right next to her ear. "You look so fucking hot, Mandy," he whispered. "With your tail up over your back and your cunt in the air. Like a bitch in heat, aren't you, just begging for it? Would you sit up and beg for me, Mandy-girl? Would you beg for my cock?"

The words hit like slaps, and humiliation washed over her. She wanted to hide, to turn her face away so he couldn't see it, couldn't see the red flush that heated her cheeks, or the lust she knew was in her eyes. Because as much as the words brought a sweeping shame that made her want to hide, they also brought the most intense, all-encompassing lust she'd ever felt.

So she forced her eyes to remain open and turned her head so she could look up into his face. His eyes were blazing, like blue fire, lit from within by lust and excitement and love. So much love for her. Even like this, with her very humanity stripped away, that love was there, bright and strong and true.

It gave her courage to see it, to feel it, and to know that no matter what, it would never go away.

"Would you?" he repeated and slid his finger deeper. His lips curled into a softly cruel smile when she whined, her hips giving a short, involuntary spasm before she controlled it, her cunt clamping down on his finger.

"Beg," he commanded softly. "Beg like a bitch in heat."

She couldn't use her words, but she could use her voice, her body, so that was what she did. Whines and whimpers spilled from her throat and she pushed her hips back into his invading finger, wordlessly pleading for more. His hand was planted on the floor by her shoulder, so she turned her head to nuzzle and lick at his fingers, his wrist. The scent and taste of his skin, of James, made her nearly frantic with need, and she battered at him with her paws.

His soft laugh was delightfully wicked. "Such a slutty little puppy I have," he crooned. "Such a needy, slutty puppy."

She whined in protest when he moved away, leaving her aching pussy empty. Her hips humped up, seeking, and he laughed again.

"Like a bitch in heat," he said, the satisfied smirk on his face making her blush once more even as her pussy clenched in reaction, then he was moving behind her.

His jeans scraped her tender inner thighs as he nudged her knees apart, the bite of his zipper cold against her heated skin. Then his cock was there, hot and hard. He dragged it across her clit, laughing when she jumped, then shoved it deep in one thrust.

She bit her lip so hard to keep from screaming that she tasted blood. God, he felt huge, the plug in her ass forcing him to make space where it felt as though there was none, and for a moment, she wasn't sure if she could take it.

She pressed her face into the rug, struggling to breathe, to adapt. Her pussy was fluttering, adjusting to accommodate his girth, her opening stretched deliciously tight around him. That was her favorite part of sex, that stretch and burn at the beginning, pain and pleasure all at once, and it was so, so good.

Then he grabbed the base of the plug and tugged, so the widest part pulled against the tight ring of muscle, and she was stretched there, too. To her utter shock, she felt the first hard flutters of an orgasm.

"Both your pretty little holes stuffed full," he said, his voice coming to her through the roaring in her ears, "and that's all it takes for my slutty puppy to come."

He pulled himself free, dragging his cock through her snug sheath while keeping the tension on the butt plug. Something cool and wet hit her overheated flesh, and she realized he was adding lube. Then he shoved forward, impaling her once more, and she screamed as she came.

He fucked her through it with cock and plug, shoving both deep before pulling them almost free, then going deep again. A second orgasm followed the first, the force and the speed of it catching her by surprise. Her body spasmed and jerked against him, the pleasure going on for so long that it became torment, but still he kept on until she was clinging to the thin edge of sanity.

Then he stiffened inside her, shoved deep one last time, and roared as he came, flooding her with come and heat and, impossibly, set off a third round of spasms. By the time he'd softened inside her, she felt half dead.

But what a way to go.

He pulled free, his cock scraping hard against her bruised and swollen cunt, and she shuddered. Then he was kneeling in front of her, his half-hard cock in hand, dripping with his come and hers. He tangled his other hand in her hair, dragging her up. "Suck me clean," he said, and she opened her mouth to obey without a thought.

She sucked gently, tasting both of them, the moment intimate and filthy in the best possible way. When he was clean, she let him go with a last, loving lick, and laid her head down on the rug again while he tucked himself back into his jeans.

"That's my good girl," he whispered, brushing her hair away from her face as she began to drift away. "That's my good girl."

* * * *

James glanced at the clock on the bedside table, then at the woman curled up at the foot of the bed. It was ten o'clock, and normally they'd just be thinking about getting ready for bed. But it had been a long, tiring day, and his puppy girl was already asleep.

God, she was cute. The ears were crooked on her head, knocked askew when she'd tucked her hands under her cheek. The mittens and booties still covered her hands and feet, and the way she was curled on her side meant he could just see the edge of the tail over her hip.

He frowned and checked the clock again. She'd worn the tail—and the plug—for most of the day without a break. He'd added lube a couple of times, wanting to make sure she didn't dry out, and he'd removed it completely after dinner. That had been so he could fuck her ass, though, and it had been promptly replaced once he'd come deep inside her clutching hole, so couldn't really be counted as a break.

He'd removed the tail from the base of the plug, and the rest of her gear, when he'd given her a bath afterward. He'd wondered if the loss of all the paraphernalia would jolt her out of puppy mode, and had been prepared to end the scene there if it had. But she'd sat quietly while he'd wet her down and soaped her up in the big walk-in shower, rubbing her head against his hand and licking the water from his wrist. And when he'd taken the hand-held nozzle to rinse her off, she'd frolicked and splashed with excited yips, and shaken herself so hard she'd fallen over. After, she'd leaned against him as he was drying her off, and sat obediently to have her ears, tail, and paws put back on. Then she'd grabbed the end of the towel in her teeth and growled, resulting in a careful game of tug-of-war and another round of orgasms.

Her delighted reaction had been a far cry from their trip to that same shower earlier in the day.

His lips twitched when he remembered the absolute outrage on her face when she'd realized that he expected her to do everything like a puppy—including pee.

He'd thought for a moment that she was going to call the scene, safeword out and be done. If she had, that would've been fine with him. He had no expectations for the exercise except to discover if she liked it, and if she didn't, then no harm done. He'd hidden his amusement at her reaction and waited patiently for her to decide what she wanted to do. She'd studied his face so intently, her eyes narrowed as she'd searched every nuance of his expression, and it had gone on so long he'd been on the verge of calling it himself.

But she'd surprised him then, lifting first one hand, then the other, so he could remove the mittens, sitting quietly while he'd slipped off the booties and knee pads and unclipped her tail from the plug. Then she'd turned and, moving carefully over the hard tile, crawled into the shower.

Her face had gotten red then, blazing red, and she'd looked away. He'd crouched down, cupping her face in both hands so she had to look at him, and waited. He could see the struggle on her face, the fight between the basic physical need to pee and the desire for the privacy she was used to. He'd kept his eyes on hers, his expression calm and his voice soft and encouraging, and after a long moment, she let go.

Her cheeks had been bright red the entire time, her skin so hot it burned under his fingertips, but there had been relief in her eyes, too, and gratitude. He'd been shocked to find himself blinking back tears, touched and moved by the trust and faith it had taken for her to expose herself so fully in front of him. He'd kissed her, soft and sweet as she'd finished, and lovingly rinsed and dried her off. He'd replaced each piece of puppy gear, whispering words of praise and pride, and by the time he was finished, her face had been glowing with quiet pleasure.

Even now, hours later, the impact of that moment hadn't faded. It had lingered throughout the day, while they played and while they rested, when he'd fed her dinner and fucked her afterward. It was there now, while she slept curled at the foot of the bed as a puppy would, her ears askew and her tail drooping, and even though he'd planned to officially end the scene at midnight, he suddenly very much wanted his wife back.

He rose quietly from the bed to walk to the bathroom for a wet washcloth and a towel, then came back to perch on the side of the bed. He pulled her booties off first, letting them fall to the floor, then tugged the headband free. She stirred, her lashes fluttering, and gave a quiet, inquiring yip that made him smile.

"Puppy time is over, Amanda," he said softly, and freed her hands. He stroked a hand down her back as she flexed her fingers, wiggling them around. "You okay?"

"Yeah," she whispered, her voice a little rusty from lack of use. "What time is it?"

"Just after ten." His hand settled on her lower back. "I have to take the plug out."

She winced, but nodded. "Okay."

"Deep breath, love," he instructed, and got a firm grip on the base. "And out."

He tugged it free when her breath whooshed out. He pressed a soft kiss to her mouth, set the plug aside for later cleaning, and picked up the washcloth.

"Stay still while I clean you up," he said, and she lay quietly until he was finished.

"What do you need?" he asked her, brushing her hair away from her face.

She sighed, turning her face into his hand. "I'm thirsty," she admitted. "And I have to pee again."

He chuckled at that, then slid off the bed and reached down to help her up. "You can do that by yourself, if you like."

The look she gave him when she stood made him laugh again. "I'm going to take that as a yes."

"It's definitely a yes," she muttered, and took a wincing step toward the bathroom.

"Joints a little stiff?" he guessed, and she nodded. "Want me to carry you?"

She shook her head. "I need to stretch a little."

"Okay. While you do that, I'll get you some water."

Her smile was sleepy, her eyes soft. "Thanks."

"You're welcome."

He waited to make sure she made it to the bathroom okay, then trotted downstairs for a bottle of water. He took a minute to shut down the house, turn off the lights and lock the doors, and by the time he made it back to the bedroom, Amanda was already climbing into bed.

She took the bottle of water gratefully and sipped steadily as he shed his clothes and slid under the covers next to her. When she'd drunk about half the bottle, she set it on the nightstand then lay down with a sigh.

"All right?" he asked.

"Hmmm." She curled up next to him, her head on his shoulder. "Tired. A little sore."

"Want a hot shower?"

She shot him a look. "Nobody's getting in that shower again until it gets scrubbed," she said drily, and he shook with laughter.

"I'll do it in the morning," he assured her, still chuckling.

"Good," she said, and yawned, and closed her eyes. "I want to sleep, now."

"Go right ahead, love. Will it bother you if I read for a while?" he asked.

She shook her head, her hair sliding over his skin. "Nope. Love you."

He leaned down to press a kiss to her hair. "Love you too, Mandy-girl," he whispered.

Her eyes stayed closed, but she smiled, and he watched her drift off to sleep. He put his book aside, no longer interested in reading, and clicked off the light. He lay in the dark, listening to her breathe, feeling it against his skin, until he drifted off, too.

Chapter Eight

James was up at his usual early hour the next morning, and true to his word, scrubbed the shower clean. When Amanda stirred a couple of hours later, stiff and sore, and declared she'd rather have a bath than a shower, he drew it for her. He saw her safely ensconced in frothy, fragrant bubbles, then took himself downstairs to make breakfast.

She wandered in, flushed and dewy from her bath, just as he was removing the last of the bacon from the frying pan.

"Mmm, bacon," she said, and crossed to the stove. She was wearing his robe again, her customary thick socks on her feet, her hair still damp from the bath. She slipped her arms around him from behind and laid her head on his back. "Hi."

"Hi," he replied, and switched the stove off before turning in the circle of her arms and looping his own around her waist. "How was your bath?"

"Lovely," she said with a sigh, and propped her chin on his chest to look up at him.

"Still sore?" he asked.

"A little," she admitted. "I wouldn't mind some ibuprofen. My knees are sore, and crawling uses different muscles than walking."

He stretched out to pull the bottle of painkillers from the cabinet above the stove and shook two out. She took them, and the glass of orange juice he handed her to swallow them down.

"Thanks." She smiled up at him. "Is breakfast ready? I'm starving."

He leaned down for a quick kiss and nudged her toward the breakfast bar, where he already had two place settings laid out. "Sit, and I'll bring it over."

She wandered over, juice in hand, while he pulled the platter of waffles and scrambled eggs out of the warming drawer. "Coffee?"

He shot her a firm look. "Not until you've drunk all your juice, and a glass of water. You're dehydrated after yesterday."

She frowned at him. "It's hard to drink from a bowl."

He stifled a grin and slid onto the stool next to her. "I know."

"Sadist," she muttered, and only sighed when he laughed.

"Eat first, call me names later," he said, and slid a waffle onto her plate.

"I can do both," she informed him as he added eggs and bacon next to the waffle.

"Believe me, I know." He filled his own plate, and, pleased to see her dig into the food, did the same.

They ate in relative silence, pausing only to refill glasses or replenish plates. She drained both her juice and her water with a flourish, then, with a hard stare that dared him to stop her, got up and poured herself a cup of coffee.

Amused, he waited until she'd settled onto her stool with a satisfied sigh. "Better?"

"Much," she declared, and took a long sip of the fragrant brew. "What's on the agenda for today?"

"Not a thing," he told her. "Today is for rest and recalibrating. I figured we could both use a day to decompress. Yesterday was a lot."

"That's an understatement," she said with a roll of her eyes.

He set aside his fork and picked up his water, swiveling on the stool to face her. "What'd you like about it?"

"Besides the orgasms?" she said with a cheeky smile.

He reached out and tweaked her nose. "Yes, besides that."

She wrinkled her nose at him, then her expression turned thoughtful. "It was more fun than I expected."

"Fun?"

"More playful," she explained. "I don't know why, but I thought it would be serious. Like, I don't know, that you'd be pretending to train me or something. I was expecting lots of commands and corrections. Although you did threaten to crate me."

"I had to have some form of punishment available," he said, biting back a laugh at her narrow-eyed stare. "But I didn't buy a crate, so it was an idle threat. This time."

"This time?"

He pinched her chin. "For this first time, I thought I'd keep things low key."

Her eyes went wide. "That was low key?"

"Low discipline," he amended.

"Oh. Yeah, that was a good call. Once I got past the kneejerk weirdness of it and started thinking of it as just another role play, it was fun."

"I'm glad. Was it humiliating?"

She frowned. "Parts of it. When you first put all the dog stuff on me, the paws and the ears, the tail…it was embarrassing. But it didn't last very long. Like I said, after a bit, it just felt like role play."

He nodded. "What else did you find humiliating?"

She grimaced, an uncomfortable look coming into her eyes, and she hesitated. He waited patiently, knowing that it sometimes took her a minute to put a voice to difficult feelings. And that when she was ready, she'd tell him, even if it was hard.

"There was a moment, when I first climbed on the couch…" she began.

"Ah." He nodded. "When I touched your breasts, and your belly. You didn't like it."

She huffed out a breath. "Not at first, no."

"Tell me why."

She grimaced again, then lifted her chin and looked him in the eye. "I don't want you to think that I think about this a lot, because I don't. I'm happy with my body."

"All right."

"But…" She frowned a little, tapping her fingers on the counter as she searched for the right words. "I'm forty-six, and my body is softer than it used to be. Normally it doesn't bother me," she hastened to assure him. "Most of the time I feel sexy and beautiful, and I know you think I am."

"You are," he said simply, and her smile bloomed.

"I know." She shrugged. "But sometimes, in certain positions, things…hang. Things that didn't used to hang, or that I think shouldn't."

"Like breasts, or bellies," he put in.

She nodded, a little sheepish. "I didn't want you to touch me, not there. Not then."

"You relaxed after a minute."

She shrugged again. "It was a kneejerk reaction. Instinctive, you know? Once I had a minute to settle, to remind myself that sagging bellies don't bother you, that you love me just as I am…it went away."

"Good. What else did you find embarrassing?"

The look she shot him now was sulfuric. "Well, peeing like a dog was pretty humiliating."

"I had a bet with myself that you'd safeword out at that point."

Her eyes bugged. "You *wanted* me to safeword?"

"No," he said, trying not to laugh outright at her expression. "But I thought if anything was going to do it, it would be that."

"I almost did," she admitted. "If you thought I'd react that strongly to it, why did you do it?"

It was his turn to shrug. "It's a pretty basic part of puppy play, and definitely one of the more humiliating aspects. Since that was the goal, it didn't seem right to exclude it."

She grumbled a little, but he could tell she saw the logic in that.

"The second time seemed easier," he prompted.

"It was," she said, though she still didn't look comfortable. "It helps that we have the walk-in shower.

If I'd had to pee on puppy pads, or if you'd had to take me outside..."

"It's below freezing outside," he pointed out. "I could hardly take you out into the snow with nothing on but booties and kneepads."

"But if it had been summer...?" she prompted.

"Then you'd have been peeing outside," he said calmly.

"Thank God for snow," she muttered.

He laughed and nudged her knee with his. "You're stalling. Tell me how it made you feel."

She flushed a little now, remembering, but her voice was strong and her gaze steady. "That's when I felt the most dehumanized. I mean, we don't go camping or hiking or any other activity where I might find myself having to pee without a toilet around, so it's not something I think about. If I have to go, I find a bathroom. It's neat, it's clean, it's civilized."

She drew in a deep breath, then let it out slowly. "If you'd been different, I don't think I'd have been able to do it."

"What do you mean?"

"You were so calm," she remembered. "You just stood there, looking at me. Waiting. You weren't mad, you weren't impatient. You weren't even stern, not really. You knew it was hard for me, and that I was struggling, and I got the feeling you'd sit there as long as it took for me to work through that, even if it took all day."

"I would have."

"If you'd yelled or threatened to punish me for moving too slow...yeah, I would've used my safeword. It would've been too much."

He reached for her hand, some of the tightness in his chest easing when her fingers twined with his. "I'm glad you didn't have to."

"Me too." She squeezed his fingers. "Anyway, the second time…well, I'd already done it once. And you'd already demonstrated that watching me pee while on my hands and knees hadn't made you want me any less."

"Just the opposite, actually."

That made her pause. "Really?"

"Really." He tugged at her hand so she slid off the stool to stand between his spread knees. "Watching you let go, knowing the trust and faith you had to have in me to do that? I've never wanted you more."

"Wow."

"Yeah." He leaned forward for a soft kiss, then drew back. "What else?"

"What else what?" she murmured, leaning in to kiss him again, and he huffed out a laugh.

"Behave, woman," he said, and punctuated the order with a firm smack on her ass. "Talk now, sex later."

"Fine." She drew back with a pout, but she was smiling. "Overall, I liked it. Once I got used to it, and comfortable, it felt like just another role play. Except I got to growl and bite you."

He chuckled at her gleeful expression. "I thought you'd like that. On a scale of one to ten, how humiliating was the experience for you?"

"The whole thing, not just the peeing in the shower?" She pursed her lips. "A four, maybe a five?"

"That's pretty low."

"Yeah." She frowned lightly. "I didn't find being a puppy humiliating, just some of the things I had to *do* as a puppy." She looked like she wanted to say something else, then suddenly stopped, a horrified look on her face.

"What?"

She shook her head. "Nothing."

"Amanda," he said sternly.

"I was just…" She huffed out a breath, her cheeks flushed with color. "I was just thinking how grateful I was that peeing was all I had to do."

He burst out laughing. "You mean…"

"Yes, I mean." She shoved at his shoulder as he continued to laugh, her cheeks bright and a reluctant smile on her lips. "I think that would have made me safeword, no matter how understanding you were being."

"Noted." He dropped a kiss onto her nose. "The parts that were humiliating, were they a turn-on?"

She hesitated. "Not really?"

"You're not sure?"

She shook her head. "We were playing, and that's always sexual for me. And knowing you're turned on turns me on. But it honestly wasn't that humiliating, and the parts that were, like the peeing…it made me feel really submissive, and I liked that, but not necessarily aroused. Make sense?"

He nodded. "Do you think any of that would change if we were doing a scene like that in public?"

"Oh, wow." She pressed a hand to her belly. "That'd be a total game changer. I'd have to think on the why of it, but right now I'll just say the idea makes me very nervous."

"Good to know," he drawled, deliberately putting a hint of evil Dom in his voice, and she smacked his shoulder again.

"I am not peeing in front of other people."

He merely smiled. "We'll see."

"And we are definitely *not* getting a crate."

"We'll see," he said again, and waggled his eyebrows to make her laugh.

"Pervert," she accused.

"That's why you love me."

She softened against him, leaning in so her breasts nestled against his chest. "That's why I love you," she agreed, and tilted her face up for a kiss.

She tasted like bacon and Amanda, sweet and soft and wonderfully familiar. He caught her close when she would've pulled back, taking the kiss deeper, sweeping his tongue into her mouth to get more of that heady Amanda taste, then drew back to nibble on her lips because he knew it drove her wild. She shivered, and he smiled against her mouth.

"You're wearing my robe again," he murmured, trailing his lips down to her earlobe.

"You gave it to me," she pointed out, her voice going breathy with arousal. Her fingers dug into his shoulders, and her pulse was pounding in her throat.

"It was a loan," he reminded her with another smack to her ass. "I want it back."

"I'm not done with it." Her protest was laced with laughter.

He spanked her again, hard enough this time to make her gasp. "I'm not asking again."

"You didn't ask the first time."

"Brat," he said, trying not to laugh, and jerked the robe off her shoulders to bare her to the waist.

"Pervert," she replied, her back arching as he pinched her nipples.

"You know what I missed yesterday?" he asked almost absently, his eyes locked on the way her nipples had tightened and darkened. He pulled on them, loving her choked gasp as he slowly, steadily, stretched them away from her body.

"What?"

"I missed seeing your face when you came." He let her nipples go, watching her breasts bounce, her strangled cry music to his ears.

Then he scooped her up, carried her to the sofa, and made her come twice, just so he could watch her face.

* * * *

On the last Saturday in January, the St. Louis Kink Club held their monthly board meeting and play party. The board meeting ran late, as usual, so by the time James and Amanda made their way to the party, it was already in full swing.

"I still think it's a better idea to hold the conference at a smaller hotel," Amanda said. "That way we can block it out entirely, and we don't have to worry that we're going to shock the tourists."

"But a smaller hotel won't have the event space we need for the parties, or enough conference rooms for all the workshops we want to offer," James pointed out.

Amanda huffed out a breath, annoyed. "Tell me why we agreed to be on the board again?"

James ran a soothing hand down her arm. "Because we care about our community and wanted to serve it."

"Right." She stepped into the play space and glanced around. The open end of the small warehouse was well lit, if a little chilly, and there were already people playing on the various pieces of equipment scattered around the perimeter of the room. The bar was set up along the far end, with a petite blonde behind it.

"Oh, Olivia's here." Amanda started forward, intent on getting a drink and catching up with her friend, then stopped. "Am I allowed to drink tonight, or are we playing?"

"We're playing," he informed her, and hefted the leather satchel that served as his toy bag to prove it. "No booze."

"Okay," she replied, not even a little disappointed that she'd be drinking soda instead of whiskey. "Is it okay if I go over and say hi?"

"That's fine." He ran an affectionate hand down her hair, then unzipped the satchel and pulled out a thin strip of black leather. "Once you're appropriately attired."

She stood quietly while he buckled the collar into place, feeling the familiar sense of calm wash over her. She didn't wear a collar in her everyday life, the way many submissives in committed relationships did, but she always wore one when they were in public kink spaces, whether they planned to play or not. The collar was a reminder to others that she was unavailable and reinforced the D/s dynamic that she had with James. It wasn't 24/7, even when they were at home, but regarding sex and kink, he was in charge, and the collar was a physical reminder of that.

He ran a finger under the leather, checking to make sure it wasn't too tight, and dropped a light kiss on her lips. "I need to check on a few things. I want you to stay in the bar area until I come find you. Clear?"

"Clear, Sir," she said. She wanted to ask what kind of scene they would be doing. She knew it wouldn't be a puppy play scene. They'd agreed to talk more thoroughly before doing it again, especially in public, but that still left a whole world of kinky possibilities.

He must have read the questions on her face, because his smile went smirky as he waggled his finger. "No questions. You'll know when you need to know."

"Yes, Sir." She said it with a pout just for form, then stretched to her toes to give him a smacking kiss. "Do I have permission to go pee if necessary?"

"Yes, you do." He hooked his fingers in the collar and gave it a short yank. "You can even use the bathroom this time."

"You're a laugh riot, Sir," she said, and remembered at the last minute that rolling her eyes at him in public fell under the heading of Very Bad Idea.

"I know." He tugged the collar again, this time pulling her closer, and kissed her. "Go. I'll find you when I'm ready."

She walked away, adding an extra swish to her hips because she knew he was watching, and grinned to herself when his soft laugh reached her ears.

She made her way through the crowd, pausing here and there to exchange friendly greetings. She stepped up to the bar, which was really just a reception desk that had been left behind in one of the warehouse's offices. But it had a fancy marble top and plenty of storage for cups and booze, so it worked.

"Amanda." Olivia beamed, her hazel eyes lighting up as she leaned over for a hug. "It's good to see you."

"You, too." Amanda returned the hug enthusiastically. "I didn't know you were tending bar tonight."

"Well, I can't play, so Kyle volunteered to DM, and signed me up to tend bar."

"Why can't you play?"

Oliva took a step back so Amanda could see past the short, snug dress to the elastic bandage wrapped around her knee. "I hyper-extended it yesterday."

"Ouch." Amanda winced in sympathy. "Are you okay?"

"Sore, but it'll be fine. It just needs rest. Elevation, ice, the usual."

"Then why aren't you icing and elevating it?" a deep voice asked, and both women jumped.

Olivia huffed out a breath, raising a hand to smooth her short sweep of honey blonde hair as she turned to glare at the man who'd somehow managed to walk up to the bar unnoticed. "How are you so quiet?"

"Talent," he said shortly. "Why aren't you sitting?"

"Because I'm in service, that's why," Olivia shot back.

Cade's normally cheerful expression folded into a scowl, his dark eyes flashing with an anger he rarely exhibited. He started to speak, then paused. Finally, he said, "Don't overdo it."

"I won't," Olivia said, clearly perplexed. "What's wrong?"

"Nothing," he ground out, then dragged a hand over his short-cropped hair. "Nothing," he said again, calmer this time. "Sorry."

"It's okay," Olivia said, her expression clearing, though there was still a cloud of confusion in her eyes. "Are we still on for game night this week?"

"Yeah." Cade smiled, though it didn't quite reach his eyes. "Wednesday night. Jason's DMing, so be prepared."

"Oh." Olivia rolled her eyes a little. "Yay."

"You know, anyone else would take that eye roll as a sign of disrespect," Cade admonished, a twinkle in his dark eyes despite his glower.

"It was," Olivia snorted. "For Jason."

Cade's grin flashed as he turned to Amanda. "Amanda, how are you?"

"I'm good, thank you, Sir," Amanda said. "How's your arm?"

Cade held up his right arm, the line of newly healed pink flesh bright against his darker skin. "Stitches are out, and I got the go ahead to play."

Out of the corner of her eye, Amanda saw Olivia frown. "That's great."

"And about time. I'm ready to climb the walls." He turned to Olivia. "I'm having someone bring you two chairs. When you're not serving, sit on one with your leg up on the other."

"But—"

"Not negotiable," he interrupted.

She huffed out a breath. "Fine."

Amanda bit back a laugh as Cade frowned. "Fine, what?"

"Fine, Sir. Thank you, Sir."

"There we go." Cade glanced at Amanda, humor dancing in his dark eyes once again. "Amanda."

"Sir." Amanda waited until he was out of earshot to turn to Olivia. "What was *that*?"

"What was what?" Olivia said, scowling after Cade.

"You two were flirting."

That had Olivia's head whipping around. "What? We were not."

"You really were." Amanda grinned. "How long has that been going on?"

"It hasn't. We're friends," Olivia insisted. "We're in the same gaming group, and we hang out sometimes, that's all. It wasn't flirting. Besides, I'm with Kyle."

"Right. How's that going?"

"Pretty good." Olivia smiled. "We moved in together last month."

"Really?" *Shit,* Amanda thought, but kept her dismay to herself. "It's good?"

"Getting there," Olivia said with a shrug. "There's always an adjustment period, you know?"

"Sure." Amanda nodded.

"Anyway, Kyle thought we should live together. He thought it would help foster intimacy."

Amanda thought drily that if intimacy wasn't there after almost a year of dating, moving in together wasn't going to make it happen. But she kept that to herself, too. "You're still working on doing CNC?"

"We haven't yet, but we're getting close."

Amanda nodded. Consensual non-consent scenes were tough, requiring intimacy and trust. She thought Olivia was going about exploring it the right way...she was just doing it with the wrong guy. "I'm happy for you."

"Thanks. What about you? How goes the shame game?"

Amanda laughed. "Shame game?"

Olivia flashed a smile, her teeth white against her bright pink lipstick. "Sadie's words, not mine."

Amanda just laughed again. "It's going fine. We haven't done anything with it since the puppy play, but I think James has something up his sleeve for tonight."

"Well, then let's make sure you're hydrated," Olivia said, and set a bottle of water on the bar.

"Thanks." Amanda twisted off the cap and took a sip. "I feel…"

"Edgy," Olivia supplied.

"Yeah." Amanda blew out a breath. "That's a good word for it."

"A good word for what?" James asked, and Amanda turned as he strode up to the bar. He laid a hand on the small of her back and smiled across the bar at Olivia. "Hello, Olivia. How are you?"

"I'm good, Sir. Thank you for asking. Can I get you anything to drink?"

He shook his head. "Not right now, thank you. Edgy is a good word for what?" he asked Amanda.

She knew better than to evade, especially here. "For how I feel right now."

His eyes lit with delight and something else, something that had a shiver running down her spine. "Are you nervous, darling?"

She forced herself not to drop her gaze. "Yes, Sir."

"Good," he said bluntly, and she nearly laughed.

"Pervert," she accused softly.

His eyes gleamed at her as he plucked the water bottle from her hand. "Go use the bathroom and meet me back here."

"Yes, Sir." She turned to walk on suddenly unsteady legs to the restrooms.

She finished as quickly as she could, then took a moment to check her appearance in the mirror. Since she had no idea what James had planned, she'd worn one of her basic, no-frills fetish outfits—short black skirt, a matching scoop-necked top, black knee-high boots. She'd chosen a bright pink lipstick for a pop of color, and left her hair in its usual sleek cap.

She wished she'd brought her purse with her so she could freshen her lipstick—she'd chewed most of it off during the board meeting. But she'd left it with her coat, so she used the tip of her pinky finger to spread what was left of the gloss over her lips. Then, with nothing more to keep her in there, left the bathroom.

She found James at the bar, frowning at a now seated Olivia. "Keep the leg elevated," he told her, and nudged the second chair someone had delivered a little closer. "And as long as you're sitting, use the icepack."

"Thank you, Sir," Olivia gave Amanda a wry smile. "They ganged up on me."

"Good," Amanda said.

James held out a hand for Amanda, drawing her to his side. "And if anyone gives you any grief about sitting, tell them to see me or Cade."

A hint of nerves crept into Olivia's voice. "Can someone let my Sir know?"

"Cade already has," James said, his voice softening at the obvious worry in her pretty hazel eyes. "He'll be by to check on you after his dungeon monitor shift is over."

"Thank you."

"Of course." James smiled at her, then looked down at Amanda. "Ready?"

"For what?"

He grinned. "For whatever I want."

Amanda just sighed. "Yes, Sir. See you later, Olivia."

"Bye."

James tugged her away, bending to murmur to her. "She'll be fine."

"I don't think Kyle is taking very good care of her," Amanda whispered back.

"It's not our business, Amanda," he began, then sighed. "But I think you're right."

"What do we do?"

"Not much we can do, except keep an eye on them."

"Cade was pissed earlier," Amanda told him as they wove through the milling crowd. "He was trying hard not to show it, but he was."

"He'd like to tear Kyle into small pieces and launch him into space," James returned. "You know how protective he can be. Although I have to say, he's taking it a bit far this time."

Amanda pursed her lips. She had her own ideas about where that protective urge was coming from, but again she kept those thoughts to herself.

"Kyle's not a bad guy," James went on. "I just don't think they're a good fit."

"Me neither. Maybe we should introduce her to some other Doms, see if—"

"Stop right there," James interrupted, and drew her to a halt. "Olivia is collared to Kyle."

"I know, but—"

"And unless she's in danger," he continued, "you are not to interfere. Understood?"

She frowned. "Define interfere. Can I talk to her? Ask her if she's okay, if she's happy?"

"Of course you can. Being her friend is always acceptable. However," he said, a thread of steel coming into his tone, "trying to fix her up with someone else while she's still collared is not. And don't pretend you don't know the difference."

She sighed. "Yes, Sir."

"Good girl. Now, are you ready to get started?"

Amanda glanced around, blinking when she realized they were standing in the corner of the room set up for medical scenes. An exam table sat in front of her. "We're doing a medical scene?"

"No, we're doing a humiliation scene, using the medical table. Strip."

She began shedding her clothes, folding them into a neat pile close to the wall where they wouldn't be in the way. While she was getting naked—and trying not to think of just what kind of humiliation scene would need an exam table—James picked up a bottle of cleaner and sprayed down the table. It was most likely unnecessary, Amanda knew, as all the equipment was cleaned when it was set up, but James liked to be thorough.

He tossed the paper towels into the trash can nearby, then stepped forward and laid his hands on her shoulders. "All right?"

She swallowed. "A little nervous."

He nodded. "I haven't told you what kind of scene I have planned for tonight. Would you like to know?"

Some of the tension coiled tight in her belly ease. "Yes, please."

He nodded. "I wanted to step up the humiliation game, so to speak."

The shame game, she thought, and might've laughed if she hadn't been wound so tight. "Okay."

He stroked down her arms and up again in a light caress. "You're no stranger to playing in public, or having sex in public, but those are usually role play scenarios. This is going to be a little different. First, there's no role here. You're not Yvette the French maid, or Miss Smith the new secretary. You're just Amanda tonight. Understood?"

"Yes, Sir," she said, and the knot in her belly tightened once more. "What about you?"

"Me?" He smiled. "I'm James, the proud, loving husband showing off my beautiful, slutty wife for the crowd."

"Crowd?"

He nodded. "Crowd. You'll be able to hear them, but not see them."

He's going to blindfold me? She swallowed hard past the sudden lump in her throat. "Okay."

"There are a couple of things I'll need help with, so some of the hands touching you won't be mine."

He must have seen her panic, because he began stroking her arms again to soothe her. "They won't do anything I haven't asked them to do, and they're not going to fuck you."

She wanted to let out a huge sigh of relief, but she couldn't seem to get air past her throat. James had invited other people to participate in their scenes before, but they'd always been punishment scenes, not sexual ones. Well, that wasn't quite true—all of their scenes were eventually sexual, but he'd never invited anyone to participate in that part before.

"Take a breath, Amanda," James ordered, and she sucked in air. "Tell me what you're thinking."

"That I'm scared," she admitted.

"I'll be with you the whole time," he assured her. "I'll never be more than three feet away, and I'll be watching everything. I've filled the DMs in on the plan, and they'll be there, as well."

She knew that was supposed to be reassuring. And if she hadn't been panicking, it might have been. "I'm still scared."

"Good scared or bad scared?"

She wanted to look away, but she couldn't. "I'm not really sure."

"Fair enough," he said soberly. "Do you trust me?"

"Yes," she replied automatically, not even having to think about it. She trusted James with her life.

"That's my girl," he said, and the approval and pride in his voice washed over her in a warm wave. "I'm not going to gag you, so you'll be able to talk. Tell me what your safewords are."

"Yellow for stop to talk or slow down, red for stop right now."

"Use them if you need them," he told her. His hands left her arms to cup her face. "I love you, Amanda. I'm proud to be your husband."

The knots in her belly eased, just a little, and she sighed. "I love you, too."

He kissed her, soft and soothing, then dropped his hands and stepped back. "Up on the table, please, and lie back."

The 'please' was automatic, she knew, a result of the impeccable manners drummed into him as a child, but in no way were the words a request—they were an order. She drew a steadying breath and obeyed.

The vinyl was cold under her bare butt, and clung to her skin, chafing as she wiggled into place. She lay down, her legs out in front of her. The table was short, so her feet and ankles poked out over the end, but not so much that it made her uncomfortable, and the built-in padding at the top made for an adequate pillow.

"Comfortable?"

She wiggled experimentally, wincing when she realized that lying flat would very quickly put a strain on her lower back. She rarely slept on her back, and when she did, she had a pillow tucked under her knees. "Being flat for a long time will probably aggravate my back."

He patted her thigh. "Thank you for telling me. Anything else?"

"No, Sir."

"Good. Sit tight for a moment while I get you strapped in."

He bent low, out of her line of sight. When he rose again, he had a flat fabric strap in his hand. "Scoot down just a bit."

She complied, the vinyl rubbing against her skin again.

"That's good. Hands at your sides."

She moved her hands to the table, tucking them slightly under her hips so they wouldn't slide off the narrow space, and he laid the strap across her belly. It was thickly padded on the side that would lie against her skin, and the fabric was something soft that wouldn't chafe if she wiggled against it.

"Nick, would you get that side?" James said, and Amanda looked up to see their friend stepping up to the other side of the table.

She smiled up at him. She hadn't seen him in a while, not since the night he'd brought Sadie and his girlfriend Rebecca over so they could go out for their monthly submissives meeting. She was fond of Nick, and even fonder of Rebecca, and she opened her mouth to offer a greeting, then faltered. He wasn't looking at her, she realized, hadn't glanced her way at all. He picked up the strap that James handed him and threaded it through the slot on the other side to yank it tight across her belly.

Her startled gasp was loud, and a little pained, but even then, he didn't look at her.

"Too tight?" he asked, but he wasn't asking her.

"Ease off just a touch," James answered, and the strap loosened a fraction. "That should do."

Nick secured it, then sidestepped up to the table and took the next strap as James handed it over. This one would lie across her arms and over her ribcage below her breasts. Nick fastened it down efficiently, once again checking with James on its placement and tightness without even looking at her and did the same with the strap positioned above her breasts.

"Hands?" Nick asked.

"I'm leaving them free, for now." James decided. "Let's get her legs."

Both men moved down the table towards her feet, and Amanda tried to relax. Bondage was nothing new for her, and this kind of bondage wasn't even that restrictive. She was strapped to the table, but she could move her hands and turn her head. Having her legs bound would immobilize her further, but that wasn't new either. She liked bondage, she reminded herself. It turned her on. Even just the little they'd done so far was having a predictable effect—her nipples were hardening, and her pussy was already wet in anticipation. She was used to all that.

What she wasn't used to was the anxiety that made her breath come short and her palms dampen. That was new and strange, and the fact that it seemed to be making her pussy wetter was even more strange.

"Amanda." A sharp tap on her calf jerked her out of her thoughts. "Raise your legs."

By his tone, this wasn't the first time he'd asked. "Sorry, Sir," she said, and lifted her legs.

A strong arm came under her knees, and she raised her head to look. Nick was holding her calves up while James fiddled with the table. *Probably getting the straps in place*, she thought, then there was a metallic shriek, and the bottom half of the table disappeared.

She jerked a little at the noise, and Nick's grip on her legs tightened. James continued to fiddle with the table, clangs and clunks sounding as he worked. Then the table jerked a little, James said, "There we go," and with one more metallic screech, a stirrup appeared.

Amanda was so shocked to see it that Nick had set her leg in it and had it strapped down before she could react. The knee brace was padded, and the same type of sturdy straps that held her torso wrapped around her leg above and below the knee. A third strap secured her foot to the footrest. Her leg was comfortably supported and completely immobilized.

A small sound of distress slipped from her lips as the other leg was similarly positioned and secured, then James was back at her side, his hand resting on her belly. He bent low, his mouth next to her ear. "All right?"

"Stirrups?" she managed faintly.

"Stirrups," he said firmly. "Give me a color."

"Green, with a bright yellow streak," she answered, and drew in a deep, hopefully steadying breath. Her legs were spread apart, not garishly so, but enough that air swirled over her exposed genitals like a cool breath. She was wet, her inner thighs slick, and to her consternation, the knowledge made her blush, which somehow made her even wetter.

"Good to know," he said mildly. "Remember, I'll be with you the whole time, even if you can't see or hear me."

"Why won't I be able to see or hear you?" she asked, panic making her voice squeak.

"Because," he said cryptically, and raised an eyebrow when she opened her mouth to protest. "Trust me?"

"Yes," she said, trembling with nerves. She did trust him, she reminded herself. That her trust felt as though it were being tested gave the scene an added edge and made her determined to prove to him that she did.

"Thank you," he whispered, and bent to brush a gentle kiss on her mouth. "I trust you to use your safewords if you need to."

She nodded slightly, knowing he meant it. It didn't matter how many people were watching or what the stakes were, she knew it wouldn't matter to him if she safeworded out of a scene. In fact, he'd be more upset if she didn't, if concern for how it would make him look made her push past what she could endure. "I will, I promise."

"All right." He brushed a last kiss over her mouth, his tongue darting out to tease and tempt, then straightened and looked past her. "Are they all set?"

She turned her head to see Nick waiting on the other side of the table. "All set."

"Let's get the brakes off."

There was a muffled thump from both sides of the table, almost simultaneous, the table shaking slightly with it, and she realized they'd unlocked the wheels. Her body tensed instinctively as it rolled slightly. Nick and James each grabbed the sides and began to push, and it picked up speed.

"James? Sir?"

"Hush." He said it almost absently, but the way he was bent slightly to push the heavy table brought his face close to hers, and she could see that he meant it. "No talking unless you need to safeword."

No talking? *Oh, God.*

Her fingertips curled on the edge of the table, clinging helplessly. Lights and faces flashed by as she was rolled through the room, snatches of conversation and speculative whispers reaching her ears as she was wheeled past. The sight of a naked woman strapped to a gynecological exam table wasn't anything new for this crowd, but it appeared to be generating some buzz.

They hit a small bump on the concrete floor, jarring the table. It was no more than a little shake, and the straps held her securely, so she was in no danger of sliding off. But it jiggled her breasts and belly and thighs, and suddenly she remembered that she was completely naked, legs spread, everything out there for everyone to see.

It's nothing new, she told herself, watching the lights flash by overhead. *You've been naked in public plenty of times. Bent over spanking benches, tied to crosses or stakes, even tied spread eagle to a bed while your husband fucks you. This isn't different.*

Except it was.

She closed her eyes. Embarrassment washed over her, heat flooding her face, and she heard James chuckle.

"Already?" he murmured, and since she didn't know what to say to that—and he'd told her not to speak—she didn't answer.

There was a short jerk as the table was brought to a halt. Amanda kept her eyes tightly closed, hiding, but she couldn't close her ears.

She heard Cade's voice, raised slightly, asking if someone understood the rules. She thought he must be doing a scene with someone nearby, but the chorus of yeses came from at least a dozen people, and they were close. She heard James quietly tell Nick to lock the wheels, and knew that they'd reached whatever their destination was. She could hear the low murmur of voices, the words indistinct, but the excitement in them was almost palpable.

There was a soft touch on her cheek. "Open your eyes, Amanda," James ordered softly, and she did.

There were lights. More than just the overhead fluorescents, shining down from the warehouse's high, unfinished ceiling—she was surrounded by them. She squinted, trying to see past the glare. They were stand lights, she realized, the ones Cade brought in from his construction company from time to time if they needed extra lighting for a demo. They flanked her, a set on either side, shining brightly onto her bound body, and embarrassment flooded her anew.

James chuckled lightly, amusement and affection and, yes, lust in the sound. "Can't hide from that," he said, loud enough for his voice to carry, and a wave of laughter swept through the crowd.

Before she could react—though what could she do, tied to a table and ordered not to speak?—James pushed to his full height. "Well, let's get started, shall we?"

He stood next to the table, still close enough for her to see, though he was far enough away to be blurry now. She'd forgotten her glasses again, and for the first time she was torn between annoyance and gratitude that she couldn't see clearly. Whatever he had planned—*and oh, he has plans*—she wasn't sure being able to see what was happening would help her.

"Can't see, can you?" he chided, then he was slipping her glasses onto her nose. "You won't be able to see much, but I want what you can see to be crystal clear."

He smiled at her, warm and wicked, and pulled a pair of black nitrile gloves out of his pocket. He pulled them on with a snap that echoed in the cavernous warehouse, even over the continuous rumble of voices, and she jerked at the sound. His smile widened, and he glanced up. "Last light," he said, and when she swiveled her head to see who he was talking to, she saw Nick dragging a stand lamp over.

It was tall, though not as tall as the construction lights, and it wasn't until Nick set it down at the end of the table next to her left foot and switched it on that she realized what it was for.

"There we go," James said cheerfully, and walked down to stand between her spread legs. She couldn't quite see him, flat on her back as she was, but with her feet in the stirrups and her pussy on full display, she couldn't imagine his gaze was anywhere else.

"That won't do," he said, disapproval clear in his voice, and she tensed, worried she'd done something wrong.

"Not you, Amanda," he said, giving her inner thigh a reassuring pat. "I just need to make a slight adjustment to the stirrups. Be a good girl and hold still while I fix this."

There was another little metallic thump and a slight jerk, then the stirrup was moving, swinging out, forcing her leg to follow. The muscles of her inner thigh burned, stretching under his hand as he pushed steadily, forcing her leg wide.

"That's better," he decided. He locked the stirrup into place and gave her thigh an approving pat before doing the same on the other side.

Amanda lifted her head slightly to look. She was spread out, far more open than she would have been for any gynecological exam, her legs so far apart that three people could've stood between them. James adjusted the lamp, moving it to the inside of her leg and aiming the light so it shone directly on her pussy. Her face flamed.

"Well, well," he purred, his voice once again carrying over the crowd. "Somebody likes being all spread out, doesn't she?"

He touched her then, and she flinched in an instinctive response that got her exactly nowhere. The straps kept her immobile, and though she could move her hips slightly, he paid her wiggling no mind as he slid one gloved finger through the slick wetness between her legs.

"Oh, yes, someone likes this a *lot.*" He held up his hand, the glove glistening in the light. "Seems like I've got a little slut on my hands, folks."

There was a rumble of laughter, voices calling out in agreement. Amanda's belly quivered, and her face heated with shame, but at the same time her cunt clenched.

Everyone was looking at her, bound and spread and helpless, and it was embarrassing and mortifying and *oh God, so fucking hot.*

James lowered his hand and this time slid two fingers into her, shoving them deep with no warning, and the moan escaped before she could stop it.

She heard him chuckle, heard the crowd laugh with him, but it was lost in a swirl of sensation. She was shocked to realize she was close to orgasm, dangerously close, and she felt a moment of panic. He hadn't told her if she was allowed to come, and while he hardly ever restricted her in such a way during private play, public play was a different story.

"I didn't tell you if you were allowed to come, did I?" he said conversationally as he fucked his fingers into her. The slick sound of his gloved fingers sliding in and out of her was loud, so loud, and she knew if she could hear it, everyone else could, too.

"I don't think you're going to be able to stop her," someone said, and she dimly recognized Cade's slow drawl. "That pussy is primed and ready to go off."

"It does look that way," James replied while the blood roared in Amanda's ears. "Are you going to come, Amanda?"

She bit her lip and struggled to keep her hips still. Oh God, she was so close. The little flutters deep within, the pressure and tension coiling tighter, harder. She didn't know if she wanted to come with all these people watching, but she was very much afraid that in a moment, she wouldn't have a choice.

"Oh, I forgot. I told you not to speak, didn't I?" James slid his fingers out, then back in again, hard enough to make her grunt. "That's all right. I don't really need an answer. I can see that you are."

He brushed his thumb over her engorged clit, chuckling when her cunt clamped down on his fingers. "Yes, you are close. You know what? I'm feeling generous tonight, love. You go right ahead and come when you're ready. And you can scream all you like."

Relief flooded through her at the words, but it didn't last long. She fought against the need to come, trying to hold it at bay, not wanting everyone to see it, but his fingers were relentless, curling forward to hit the front wall of her cunt with every thrust, and when his thumb pressed down hard on the top of her clit, she lost the battle.

She pulled against the restraints, gritting her teeth as the contractions hit, hard pulses that he pushed through with stabbing fingers. He fucked her through the orgasm until she went limp, still and sweaty on the now slick table.

"Nice," she heard someone say, and realized with a jolt that it was Nick's voice. "She always come like that?"

"Usually she's a little more vocal," James told him, "but I think she's feeling a bit self-conscious tonight."

Nick's laugh was low and wicked. "Tough to blame her. At least thirty people saw that slutty little display."

"Oh, she likes being on display," James replied, and patted her swollen pussy.

"She must," Cade put in as shame washed over Amanda once again. "I've never seen anyone come that fast just from being fingerfucked."

"Well, she's a slut," James replied easily.

"Hmmm. How fast do you think she can come again?" Cade asked.

"We'll see, won't we?" James said with a wicked chuckle. "Bring me the machine."

Chapter Nine

James kept an eye on Amanda as the fucking machine was wheeled over. She was still flushed and dewy from the orgasm, but her mouth had tightened, and her eyes were darting back and forth behind her glasses, trying to see what was going on. He laid a hand on her inner thigh, and her muscles vibrated like the plucked strings of a violin.

"I'm not going anywhere," he said quietly, for her ears only.

She relaxed fractionally, though she was still looking around, and he realized she couldn't see him through the glare of the lights.

"Give me a color," he said. He hadn't intended to ask, but she looked so scared, and he knew the question, and the reminder that he was still paying attention, would calm her down.

"Green," she whispered, and her breath rushed out on a sigh. Her face relaxed, the tightness around her mouth and eyes easing, and the muscles under his hand stopped quivering.

"If it changes, let me know," he said, and patted her as Nick and Cade pushed the fucking machine between her legs.

He held up a hand, then jerked his head in a signal he'd prearranged with both men. They nodded and moved to the head of the table, Cade crouching under to access the mechanism that would allow the head of the table to be raised while Nick loosened the straps across Amanda's abdomen and torso. James kept his hand on her thigh, as much for comfort as for restraint, while Nick helped Cade slowly raise the top half of the table so Amanda sat in a reclining position that would allow her to see what was happening.

She looked around, still nervous but curious now. Cade and Nick locked the table back into place and began to re-secure the straps. She frowned a little as she looked down between her spread knees, and James realized he was blocking her view. He stepped out of the way and had to bite back a grin at how her eyes widened when she saw what stood between her legs.

The fucking machine was made of stainless steel that gleamed under the lights, and the fake cock anchored to the end was a bright, vibrant blue. It was short, just five inches long, but it was fat. He'd ordered one that was a quarter of an inch wider than her biggest vibrator, and though it didn't seem like much, she'd feel the difference.

Cade and Nick finished strapping her down, then moved back to her head. Cade planted a hand on her forehead, making her yelp in surprise, and Nick laid a strap across her forehead. Her throat worked as Cade fastened it on the opposite side, then both men moved away, without having said a word to her.

James waited until her eyes were back on him, worry shining delightfully behind the lenses of her glasses. He waited a beat before turning to Nick.

"She's never had a fucking machine before," he said conversationally. "How do you think she'll react?"

"That greedy cunt?" Nick asked with a chuckle, his voice pitched so the crowd—and Amanda—could clearly hear. "She'll fucking love it."

"Jesus, that's a fat fucking cock," Cade said, skeptical and amused all at once. "You sure she can take it, James?"

"Oh, she'll take it," James purred.

Nick grunted in agreement. "That pussy is sloppy wet, and look, her clit's already poking out again. I got five bucks that says she sucks it right in and begs for more."

Cade shook his head, his eyes glued between Amanda's open legs. "I don't take sucker bets," he finally decided, and took a step back.

As the chatter continued around them, James picked up a bottle of lubricant from the floor and pumped some into his palm. He kept his eyes on Amanda while he moved to the silicone cock and coated it with a generous hand. He could see the signs of arousal in her, as clear as if they had neon arrows pointing the way. Her nipples were beaded tight, their color darkened with the rush of blood under her skin, and her entire chest was bright pink. Her lips were parted, the bottom one bearing dents from her teeth, and she bit into it again. Her hips were shifting, moving the scant inch allowed by the straps, pushing against the restraints.

Seeking, he knew, something that would ease the growing ache in her pussy.

Her eyes still held nerves, and the shadow of shame, but he'd wager they were adding to her arousal rather than detracting from it.

Perfect.

He slicked up the dildo until it was glistening, wiped his gloved hands on the towel Nick handed him, and stepped back. Cade and Nick flanked the machine, wheeling it closer until the dildo barely nudged Amanda's open pussy. It was a little too high, so they paused to adjust it, then at James's nod, continued forward.

Amanda's indrawn gasp echoed through the suddenly quiet space, and James realized everyone was holding their breath. His voice, when he spoke, rang out loud and clear.

"Look at you," he said, watching the wide head of the fake cock split her pussy open. A quick glance at her face showed that she was indeed looking, lust and awe gleaming in her eyes as she stared down between her legs. "You're so eager to get fucked, your slutty pussy is just opening right up for that thing."

Nick and Cade nudged the machine forward another fraction, then stopped, and James eyed it critically.

The head was lodged inside, the slick, pink skin of her cunt spread tight around it. The slightly wider shaft would spread her even farther as it fucked into her, stretching that already taut skin even more.

"Your pretty little hole is stretched wide open," he said softly, remembering how she'd reacted to that word so many weeks ago, when they'd started on this unexpected journey. She blushed, her teeth sinking so hard into her lip he wouldn't have been surprised to see blood.

"Greedy little fuck hole," he said again, just to watch her flinch, and flush, and jerk in an instinctive attempt to get more of it inside her.

"Fuck, that's hot," Cade muttered, and James knew he wasn't just saying it for Amanda's sake. "Fuck that fat cock into her, James, and let's see what that slutty cunt can do."

"Forward a little more," James said, and they nudged it forward. "Good. That'll keep that cunt stretched wide."

He picked up the controls and stepped away so he wasn't blocking the view, positioning himself next to the construction lights. He could see Amanda clearly, but she wouldn't be able to make him out in the wash of light. He hit the switch.

The dildo slid soundlessly forward, gliding slow and smooth on its track, pushing past the tightly stretched opening with inexorable force. Amanda wiggled in the restraints, panting as she struggled to adjust to the slick, thick invasion. He thumbed the button to pause the program, leaving it lodged deep inside, and waited, watching her carefully. When she relaxed fractionally and the pinched look left her eyes, he thumbed the remote.

The dildo withdrew at the same easy pace, pulling back so the head was lodged just inside her opening again, then advanced. Back and forth, slow and steady, until it was sliding smoothly all the way in and out. The plump, swollen lips of her labia clung to the shaft when it moved, but she'd adjusted to the girth enough that it was no longer dragging at her flesh, and her face held no discomfort.

He clicked the remote and the dildo sped up. Within minutes Amanda went rigid, the cords on her neck standing out as she strained against the forehead strap. Her chest flushed a dark red, and she came with a deep groan, thighs shaking and hips jerking while the silicone cock continued its steady thrusting in and out.

He stopped the machine when she lay quiet once again. He gestured to Nick and got his friend's subtle nod in return.

"Damn, she comes quick," Nick said. His tone somehow managed to be admiring and sneering all at once. "Look at that pretty pink fuck hole."

"She's greedy as fuck," Cade put in.

Murmurs of agreement came from the people who'd crowded around to watch the show. While Nick and James had been busy securing Amanda to the table, Cade had instructed those assembled on the rules of the scene, and they'd taken the 'be as verbal as you like' instruction to heart.

James glanced at Amanda, at the dying flush on her face as her eyes fluttered open. She was coming down, starting to tune into her surroundings again. He waited to see how the words would hit her.

Amanda's head was spinning. Her body felt flushed and heavy, lethargy from the orgasm dragging at her limbs. If she'd had to keep herself upright, she thought she might've crumbled to the floor, so she was grateful for the table and stirrups doing the job for her. Sweat slicked her skin, her heart thundered so hard she could almost hear the beat, and incredibly, she was still almost unbearably aroused.

"...pink fuckhole," she heard, and jerked at the words.

She couldn't move her head, but she darted her gaze about, trying to see who'd said them. The voice was familiar, but she couldn't focus, couldn't concentrate enough to discern who it was.

"Greedy as fuck," someone else said, and her belly tightened again in that top-of-the-rollercoaster feeling she recognized as shame.

Words began to filter through, coming from all around her.

Such a slut.

Spread wide open for everyone to see. Shameless!

She likes everyone watching, doesn't she?

Oh yeah, she fucking loves it. On display for everyone to see.

She took that fat cock as easily as a finger. So greedy.

So wet I could hear the dildo squish.

The words hit her like blows, slaps that stung and humiliated and incredibly, aroused. She wiggled on the table, feeling like a fish on a skewer with the dildo still lodged just inside her. The friction made her gasp, blushing furiously as the crowd laughed, then she groaned again when the dildo began to thrust once more.

It was cool at first, and she dimly realized someone must have added fresh lube. Then she stopped thinking.

The dildo battered her swollen cunt as people continued to talk, words like *slut* and *shameless* and *greedy little fuck hole* washing over her, adding to the shame in her mind and the lust in her belly.

It took longer this time, but when the dildo began moving in short, sharp jabs, she came again, her strangled cry mixing with the cheers of the crowd.

Through the cheers, she heard James laugh. "Again," he said in his dark, wicked voice, and the dildo began its slow, steady thrusting once more.

And through it all, she heard the words. *Slut. Shameless. Greedy, needy little fuckhole.* They swirled through her mind, settled in her breasts and her cunt, adding weight and heat and the sharp sting of shame.

I can't possibly come again, she thought over and over, and over and over her body proved her wrong.

She was fucking gorgeous. She'd come five times, the machine driving relentlessly into her, pushing her past what she'd believed her body to be capable of. He'd reapplied lube after each orgasm, but he wasn't sure it was enough anymore. Her pussy was swollen, battered and bruised by the relentless pounding of the machine. She'd been on the table for over an hour, and he knew he'd have to call it soon. She was drenched in sweat, her hair plastered to her skull and her skin slippery with it. Nick had checked the straps holding her in place and murmured in James' ear that they were sliding too much against her skin, and starting to chafe.

He would have to call it soon, but he wanted one more.

One more chance to hear her cry out with pleasure so intense it bordered on pain, one more chance to hear the crowd cheer as she did so. The murmurs around him had taken on an awe-filled quality, no longer sneering at the dirty slut, the shameless hussy, but admiring. Envying. He'd seen more than one submissive watching Amanda with yearning envy, and he suspected the next time the fucking machine made an appearance, there would be no lack of volunteers.

He'd kept himself from touching her, his hand on the control his only physical contact with her, but he stepped forward now. He could smell her, sweat and lube and the musky scent of her sex that had long ago obliterated any hint of the perfume she'd applied earlier. She was stripped down to flesh and need, trembling with it, and the need to touch her, to feel it sing through her, was overwhelming.

He leaned over her and laid his hand low on her belly. Her muscles quivered under it, her hips jerking as the dildo pounded home. He cupped her face with his other hand, and her eyes fluttered open to latch on to his.

"James," she managed, her voice hoarse and barely there. She strained toward him, pushing her face into his hand.

"You're so beautiful, Amanda," he whispered to her, bending close so only she could hear. "So fucking gorgeous, getting fucked for everyone to see. They can see your greedy little cunt sucking on that fat cock, they can see your clit standing out when you come. They hear you moan, and they know you're just a greedy little slut with a greedy little hole."

"James," she said again, her glasses sliding down her nose as her eyes begged him. "Please."

"You want to come again, love?" He leaned close enough to skim his tongue over her lips, tasting the salt of sweat and the sharp tang of copper, and knew she'd bitten her lip hard enough to make it bleed. "Is that what you want?"

"Please," she said again, her breath coming in sharp pants. "I can't. I can't…"

She'd already come so many times that she couldn't quite get there again, he realized. Everything was swollen, over-sensitive. She'd need more.

"It'll hurt," he warned her, his voice full of tender menace.

"I don't care," she said, raw, desperate need coming off her in waves. "Please."

"All right." He straightened and jerked his head at Nick and Cade. He'd thought this might happen and had asked his friends to lend a hand if it did. At his nod, they stepped up to either side of her, on the outside of her spread legs, and waited for his signal.

"You filthy, greedy slut," he said, and lifting his gloved hand, slapped the breast nearest to him. Almost simultaneously, Nick and Cade slapped the insides of her thighs. Her eyes went wide with shock, her short scream ringing in the open space.

He didn't pause, didn't hesitate, bringing his hand down on her other breast before the sound from the first slap had even faded away.

"Greedy slut," he said again, and slapped the first breast again. "You've already come five times, in front of all these people, and you want to do it again. Don't you? Don't you?"

"Yes," she said, half sob, half scream. "Hit me again, please. *Please.*"

Delight filled him as she begged, pleading with eyes and words, and he gave her what she wanted. Over and over, slapping both breasts at the same time while Nick and Cade continued to pepper her inner thighs with blows.

"Come on," he urged. Her chest had flushed a deep, dark pink, her nipples going even darker, and her breath was beginning to stutter. "Come on, you slut. You greedy, filthy, cock-hungry slut. Come. Come on that fat cock, come while I smack your tits, while my friends beat your thighs, spread wide so everyone can see you get fucked. Come on, baby, show me how bad you want it. Show me what a greedy, slutty, fuck hole—"

Her scream cut him off, sounding as though it had been ripped from deep within as her body convulsed. He stopped slapping her tits, laying his hand back on her belly so he could feel the contractions, the spasms and pulses of the orgasm as it hit, making her shudder and shake. Nick and Cade had stopped slapping her thighs and stepped back, leaving her wide open to the crowd, the machine still fucking steadily into her while she came.

He pulled the remote out of his pocket, fumbling to shut it off, then passed it to Cade with a jerk of his chin. Nick and Cade stepped forward and pulled the machine back, tugging it completely free of Amanda's body for the first time in over an hour, and this time her cry was one of discomfort.

"Shhh, baby." He stripped the gloves off his hands, letting them fall to the floor. He cupped her face, stroking her skin, her sweat-soaked hair, as he nuzzled her mouth. "Shhh, I'm here. It's all over. You were such a good girl, Amanda, such a good slut for me. Just hold on, okay baby? We'll get you undone, and I'll take you home."

"James." Her eyes were barely open, her face slack with exhaustion. "Love you."

He pressed a kiss to her soft mouth, then reached for the straps holding her down. "I love you, too, baby. Just hold on. Just hold on."

Chapter Ten

Oliva stared at Amanda, her jaw slack with shock. "Six orgasms?"

Amanda rolled her eyes. "It's not as great as it sounds. By the third one they were pretty much forced, and the last one nearly killed me. I didn't even wake up when James carried me to the car."

"Still," Olivia said, her hazel eyes wide. "I think my record for orgasms in a single night is three. And by 'single night' I mean *all* night. What's yours, Rebecca?"

Rebecca, a voluptuous brunette and Nick's submissive, shook her head, making her ponytail dance. "I have no idea. You'd have to ask Nick."

"Ask Nick what?" the man in question asked, coming into the room. He was tugging a sweater over his head, his blond curls in disarray, looking like he always had—like a gilded, grumpy god.

Until his eyes lit on Rebecca. Then he looked like a gilded, giddy god.

"I can't get used to you smiling all the time," Amanda told him, and brought her wine to her lips to hide her smirk when he looked at her.

"I don't smile all the time," he protested, still smiling.

Sadie came in from the kitchen and snorted. "Yes, you do. It's unnerving."

"Your friends are mocking me," Nick told Rebecca, trying to look grumpy and failing miserably.

Rebecca tilted her head back to beam at him from her spot on the sofa. "They mock with love," she told him. "Now go away."

Now he did scowl. "I don't see why I have to leave."

"Because this is a submissives' packing party, and you're not invited," Rebecca told him.

He glanced around the room. "Is this all of you? I thought Sam was coming."

"I invited him, but he had to work. He got the job in the ER that he wanted, but he had to take the night shift."

"Too bad. He'd probably keep you all in line."

"Please." Sadie snorted into her wine. "Like the awesomeness in this room can possibly be contained."

Nick turned to grin at her. "One of these days, little miss mouthy, you're going to meet a Dom who'll beat the SAM right out of you."

"The ones who want to beat it out of me never get the chance," Sadie replied with a smirk, confident in her ability to retain her smart-ass masochist status. "Now, shoo."

"Shoo?" Nick said, goggling while Rebecca tried not to laugh, and Olivia and Amanda grinned. "Shoo?"

"Shoo," Sadie repeated firmly, and punctuated the order with a wave of her hands that made the pile of ginger hair on top of her head wobble. "Go play with your big domly friends or something."

"There," Amanda said, and pointed at Nick's face, now set in a firm scowl. "That's the Nick I know."

"If you leave, you won't have to help me pack up the kitchen," Rebecca reminded him.

"Fine, I'm going." He leaned over the back of the couch and grabbed her ponytail. He gave it a yank, pulling her head backward and planting a thorough kiss on her mouth that had the room erupting in hoots and whistles.

When he lifted his head, Rebecca was flushed and Nick looked smug. "Get the kitchen packed up, and I'll fuck your ass when I get home," he told her.

"Yes, Daddy," she said with a dreamy sigh, and he laughed.

"Bye, ladies."

"Bye, Nick," they chorused as he walked out of the door, still smiling.

"You guys are so cute," Olivia said. "It's nice."

"It is nice." Rebecca's dreamy expression had yet to fade. "I just hope we're not rushing things, moving in together so fast."

Amanda shrugged and reached for a slice of cheese. "James and I moved in together after six weeks."

"I didn't know that," Olivia said.

"We'd have gotten married then, too, but I made him wait." She looked at Rebecca. "Don't worry about what people will think. If it feels right, go with it. But I do advise keeping your own bank account."

"You and James don't combine finances?" Olivia asked.

Amanda picked up her wine. "We have a joint account for shared expenses, like the mortgage, vacations, things like that, that we both put money into every month. But my paycheck, meager though it may be, goes into an account in my name."

"How's that work with your D/s dynamic?" Sadie asked, settling onto the couch next to Rebecca.

"Our D/s is mostly related to sex or play," Amanda explained, "and we keep it out of the money end of things on purpose. I need to be his equal there."

Olivia had a frown on her pretty face. "Don't you trust him?"

"Of course, I do." Amanda leaned back in her chair, wine in hand. "But I'm also a realist. James understands. His mom really struggled financially after his parents split up, mostly because his dad was a complete asshole about it. But it made him hyper aware of how much more power a man can have, even now. He insisted we have a prenup, and had it drafted specifically to make sure if we split up that I get an equal share of all marital assets, even though he makes more money and contributes more." She smiled. "He says he doesn't want any power I don't freely give him, anyway."

"But isn't that like planning for a divorce?" Olivia asked over the chorus of sighs.

"Not any more than buying car insurance is planning for an accident," she replied. "It's a just-in-case measure. I doubt I'll ever need it, but I'm happy that it's there nonetheless."

"Smart," Rebecca agreed as Olivia continued to frown. "Nick and I are keeping our finances separate for now. I told him if we ever decided to make things official, we'd revisit it."

"You brought up marriage?" Sadie nearly choked on her wine. "What'd he say to that?"

Rebecca smirked. "He said, 'fine, but we're keeping 'obey' in the vows' and bent me over the back of the couch."

Sadie sighed. "Dammit, that's kind of romantic."

"It was," Rebecca agreed, the dreamy look back on her face.

Amanda laughed and raised her glass. "Here's to romance."

"To romance," the others chorused, and clinked glasses.

"Speaking of which," Sadie put in. "I want to hear more about the Shame Game."

"Oh, me too," Rebecca said gleefully. "Besides all the awesome orgasms, how's it going?"

"It's going good," Amanda replied, smiling at the eager faces turned her way. Except Olivia, who still wore a faint frown. "We're having fun."

"I don't think I could do humiliation play," Sadie put in. "Not at that level. That scene the other night looked intense."

"It was," Amanda assured her. "But in a good way."

"Sorry, I'm not caught up," Rebecca put in. "This is kind of an experiment, right? To see how you like erotic humiliation?"

"More or less," Amanda replied. "I mean, I think it's safe to say I definitely like it at this point. But…"

"But?" Sadie prompted.

"It's a matter of degrees for me." Amanda pursed her lips and searched for the right words. "Some of the things we've done have hardly been humiliating at all."

"Like?"

Amanda turned to Olivia. "Like the puppy play."

"Wait." Rebecca held up a hand. "You didn't find puppy play humiliating?"

"Not really. It was fun, kind of silly. Well, except for the peeing part."

"The peeing part?" Olivia echoed.

"Puppies do not use toilets," Amanda told her soberly, then burst out laughing at the look of horror on her friend's face. "It really wasn't that bad."

"How did you do it?" Sadie wanted to know.

"We have that big walk-in shower in our bathroom," Amanda said with a shrug. "So, I just crawled in there and peed."

Olivia still looked horrified. "And that wasn't humiliating?"

"Oh, it was," Amanda assured her. "Especially at first. I've discovered when it comes to peeing, I very much want to remain human."

Sadie raised a hand. "Same."

"But James...he made it okay." She smiled softly as she remembered. "He didn't snap or yell or scold. He just waited, patiently, and I could see he was proud of me."

"Proud of you for peeing," Sadie put in, deadpan, and Amanda laughed.

"Yeah, like any Dom would be proud of a submissive for doing something hard and out of their comfort zone."

"Huh."

Amanda looked at Rebecca. "What?"

"It's just...that's kind of romantic, too."

Amanda nodded in perfect understanding. "Yeah, it is."

"I need more wine," Olivia muttered, and rose from the floor to go into the kitchen.

Amanda stared after her. "Is she all right?"

Sadie lowered her voice. "I think she's having some problems with Kyle, but she won't talk about it. I've tried, she just shakes me off."

"I don't like them together," Rebecca murmured. "I know I'm new around here and I can't put my finger on why, but I just don't like it."

"Me neither," Amanda said. "I wish Cade would get off his butt and make a move already."

"You think Cade is into her?" Rebecca's eyes were wide. "I mean, I know they're friends, but do you think there's more to it than that?"

"He wants there to be," Sadie put in. She darted a glance at the kitchen doorway. "I overheard him say something to Jack once."

"What?" Amanda leaned forward. "When?"

"Last October, at the monthly party. I was coming out of the bathroom, and they were in that little alcove we use for storage, and didn't see me. Bottom line? He'd move on her in a heartbeat if she was single, but he won't trespass. As long as she's with Kyle, he's keeping his distance."

"Damn," Rebecca muttered.

Sadie looked at the kitchen doorway again. "They hang out all the time, though, so I have hope. You know how they're in the same gaming group together?"

Amanda nodded. "Yeah."

"Well, I keep thinking one day they'll look at each other over the dice and just rip each other's clothes off."

Rebecca snorted. "That's asking a lot of a pair of dice."

"I know." Sadie wrinkled her nose in thought. "I wonder if strip D&D is a thing."

"It very much is not," Rebecca told her soberly.

The trio was laughing when Olivia came back in, wine bottle in hand. "What are we talking about?"

"Still on the puppy play," Sadie put in without missing a beat. "Which I definitely would have found humiliating."

"It would've been more embarrassing if we'd been in public, or had other people around," Amanda continued, picking up the thread. "But I think for me, humiliating depends on James."

"What do you mean?"

"Well, the first night we did it, when we sort of fell into it by accident? He was really distant. Not cold," she mused, "but detached, removed. I didn't feel connected to him, you know?"

"And that's humiliating?" Olivia wanted to know.

"Not by itself, no." Amanda struggled to explain. "It's like the puppy play. It's embarrassing, but he was right there, guiding me through it. Turns out, I can take a lot as long as James is with me."

"Aw," Rebecca put in.

"Double aw," Sadie added. "What about the fucking machine?"

"Well, I knew he was there, and he'd promised that he'd stay close, and that helped. But with the lights on, I couldn't see him, and he didn't touch me at all until the end. And being on the medical table..." Amanda trailed off, trying to find the right words.

"That's a mind fuck all on its own," Sadie put in.

"Yes."

"Then all those people were calling you names," Olivia said.

"What names?" Rebecca wanted to know.

Amanda smiled. "Slut, greedy cunt, filthy fuck hole. Stuff like that."

"Demoralizing," Rebecca said with a nod.

"And definitely humiliating. But also, hot." Amanda blew out a breath. "I really liked it."

"People thought James was going to let everyone fuck you," Olivia said quietly.

"Really?" Amanda blinked. "James told me after that everyone had been told what the rules were for participating."

Olivia shrugged. "I heard people talking, that's all."

Rebecca looked thoughtful. "Would you have been okay with that?"

"No." Amanda sipped her wine. "We've done threesomes before, but James has never been a pass-his-submissive-around kind of Dom. We'd probably spend six months talking about it before he'd even consider it a possibility."

"He talks to you about the kind of scenes he wants to do?"

Amanda glanced at Olivia, who was frowning again. "Not always. I mean, we have our regular scenes, stuff we do all the time, and he doesn't check with me on those. But with new stuff, like this experiment—"

"The Shame Game," Sadie put in with a grin.

Amanda laughed, then turned back to Olivia. "With new stuff, we talk. A lot. Especially something like this, that could be triggering or damaging."

Sadie sent Olivia a worried look before turning back to Amanda. "What's next on your Shame Game to-do list?"

"We've done dehumanization and public display, so that leaves objectification."

"No degradation?" Rebecca asked.

Amanda shook her head. "We took it off the table, at least for now. It feels like varsity level play, and we're still on the scrimmage team."

"How does he plan to objectify you?" Sadie wanted to know. "And when?"

"I'm pretty sure Valentine's Day is the when."

"How do you know?" Sadie asked.

"Because he asked if I could get the day off," Amanda said. "He wouldn't do that if we were just going out to dinner. Plus, he's been spacing out the scenes, so we have plenty of opportunity to talk them out and evaluate how we feel about them, and the timing is right."

"What a romantic," Olivia said with a small smile.

"And as for what," Amanda continued, "My guess is he's going to use me as a come dumpster."

"A come dumpster?" Sadie echoed.

"You know, a substitute for his fist," Amanda elaborated. "Not caring about my pleasure or comfort, just getting his and moving on."

"So, detached again," Rebecca said. "Emotionally, anyway."

"Yep."

"How do you feel about that?"

Amanda grinned at Sadie. "Hot. I feel hot."

Rebecca laughed. "Okay then."

There was a moment of silence as all four women pondered that, then Sadie clapped her hands. "Okay, this is turning me on, and I put my vibrator on the charger before I came over, so let's get this show on the road so I can get home to Mr. Buzzy. What are we packing?"

"The kitchen," Rebecca said over the peals of laughter, and pushed to her feet. "Nick tried to put all my good dishes in one box with a single sheet of bubble wrap around the whole stack, then got pissy when I told him he was doing it wrong."

"Hence, the promise of a celebratory butt fuck if we get it done." Sadie stood with a nod. "Let's go."

Amanda stood, tugging Olivia with her. "I need something to soak up this wine. How does everyone feel about pizza?"

"Already ordered." Rebecca held up her phone. "Twenty minutes."

"Have I mentioned that I really like you?" Amanda asked.

Rebecca grinned. "And I made fudge brownies for dessert."

"Hot damn!" Sadie sprinted into the kitchen. "Dibs on the corner piece!"

"They're for dessert, Sadie," Rebecca called after her.

"Not if I get to them first," Sadie yelled back.

"*Really* like her," Amanda said as Rebecca rushed into the kitchen after Sadie, and linked arms with Olivia. "Hey. You know you can talk to me, right? About anything."

"I know." Olivia laid her head on Amanda's shoulder, just for a moment, then straightened with a determined smile. "I have to work it out for myself first."

"Fair enough." Telling herself to be content with that, Amanda gave her friend's arm a squeeze. "We better hurry up or they're going to eat all the brownies."

Olivia's smile warmed, and a hint of mischief glinted in her hazel eyes. "If Sadie eats my brownie, I'll just go next door and unplug Mr. Buzzy."

"Don't you dare!"

The outraged gasp from the kitchen had both women giggling as they trooped into the kitchen to join their friends.

* * * *

Amanda woke on Valentine's day with a yawn and a stretch, then sat up. The still-drawn curtains meant the room was dim, and the clock told her it was after ten. She yawned again and slid out of bed.

She went through her morning routine—she appreciated her toilet so much these days—and was washing her hands when she saw the note.

She blinked her still bleary eyes at the sheet of paper taped to the mirror, and, fumbling a pair of glasses out of the vanity drawer—James had taken to stashing them around the house—leaned forward to read it.

Amanda,

When you wake up, take a shower. Use the shower gel I bought you for your birthday last year, and the lotion that came with it – both are on the vanity. After your shower, put on my blue robe again – don't get too excited, it's still just a loan – then go downstairs. Breakfast is waiting for you in the warming drawer. When you're finished eating, go downstairs into the large guest bedroom, strip, and put on the cuffs I've laid out for you. You may make any other preparations you feel might be necessary. I'll be home by noon, and I'll expect you to be in that room, naked, cuffed, and kneeling, ready for me.

When I come into the guest room, you will not be my beloved wife, Amanda. You will be my fuck toy. A come dumpster, a thing for me to use as I see fit. Your pleasure, your comfort, are not my concerns. They mean nothing to me. You are merely a masturbatory tool, a substitute for my fist. If I want to fuck one of your holes, I will, without regard for your pleasure or comfort. If I want to beat you, I will, and you'll take it without complaint. You will not speak a word or utter a sound. Toys don't speak, or whimper, or cry, and today, you are nothing but a toy. A thing to be used, then dismissed when I'm finished.

If you agree to these terms, text me the words "fuck toy". If for any reason you don't want to do this, text me your safeword, and we'll talk when I get home.

Either way, Amanda, I love you, and I'm proud to be your Dom.

Your loving husband,

James

"Oh." Amanda pressed a hand to her chest. "He really is a romantic."

She sighed, blinking back sentimental tears, and read the note again. This was the scene she'd predicted to her friends a couple of weeks ago, and as she'd also predicted, it was really hot. She was breathless just reading about it, her breasts growing heavy and her cunt dampening as anticipation built. There was anxiety too, the basic nerves she felt at the beginning of any scene, compounded and heightened by the fear of the unknown.

But she wasn't scared at all. She smiled at her reflection in the mirror, then, with the note in hand, went back into the bedroom. She slipped the note carefully into her nightstand where she'd be able to pull it out and read it again. She picked up her phone to send the required text before heading into the shower.

She took her time, lathering up with the shower gel that she hoarded like a miser hoarded gold, the sweet scent of honeysuckle filling the room. She scrubbed her skin pink, then stepped out and smoothed the lotion on.

She wrapped herself in the blue robe, snuggling into the thick cashmere with a sigh, then made her way downstairs.

Breakfast was scrambled eggs with cheese and sausage, and there was a full pot of coffee. She allowed herself one cup before switching to water. She didn't think a fuck toy would be offered much of a chance to rehydrate.

At eleven forty-five, she went downstairs.

Both downstairs bedrooms were furnished both for guests and for use during play parties, and all the furniture had been carefully selected with both types of use in mind. The larger of the two rooms held a platform bed of iron and wood, the sturdy posts and narrow slats perfect for bondage, and the extra thick mattress was both luxuriously comfortable for sleep and high enough to bend someone over for a solid spanking and or fucking.

The cuffs James had mentioned were on the bed, along with her favorite dildo, a brand-new ball gag, and the pump bottle of lube from James' nightstand.

If I want to fuck one of your holes, I will, without regard for your pleasure or comfort.

She eyed the large bottle of lube while the words from the note ran through her head. Anal play was something they both enjoyed, but she didn't really think he'd fuck her dry, even with the threat. He never had before, even in the roughest of scenes, and it would likely cause him significant pain as well as her. But with the scene parameters he'd laid out, she decided a little insurance couldn't hurt.

She shed the robe, letting it fall to the floor, then slipped into the bath. The last thing she wanted to do was have to safeword due to a full bladder, so she took care of that and washed up before going back into the bedroom to put on the cuffs.

They slipped on with familiar ease, metal clacking dully as she buckled them in place. They'd been used so many times she didn't even have to guess at how tight to make them—the hole punched in the leather was well worn, and easy to manage with just one hand. She sat on the edge of the bed to put the ankle cuffs on, then stood and picked up the bottle of lube.

It was cold and slick against the tender, heated pucker of her asshole, making her flinch a little. She used her index finger to push the thick, viscous liquid past the ring of firm muscle. The initial twinge of discomfort eased almost immediately, her anus fluttering as it adjusted to the invading digit. Familiar heat flooded through her as she pushed the lube deep, then returned for more. She wanted to be sure there was enough to accommodate James' cock, or whatever toy he decided to use, without too much discomfort. Using two fingers now, she pushed more lubricant in, scissoring them to stretch and prepare the delicate opening as best she could, though it wouldn't be enough to eliminate discomfort entirely. Fingers helped, and a plug would help more, but the truth was nothing fully prepared her for the stretch and burn of a cock forcing its way into her asshole.

Which, luckily, was the thing she liked about it.

She pulled her fingers reluctantly from her anus. She had enough lube in place to mitigate the pain of penetration, and though she was really tempted to continue to play, the clock on the wall told her it was nearly noon.

She started to set the bottle of lube aside, then squirted some on the fingers of her other hand and slipped them down to her pussy. She was already slick with arousal, but a little extra never hurt. She quickly swiped her hand over her swollen labia and down to the tender opening of her cunt. She shivered at the contact and would've continued if a glance at the clock hadn't warned her that time was ticking down.

She washed her hands and hurried back out to pick up the robe. She hung it on the hook on the bathroom door, then rushed to the side of the bed that faced the door and sank to her knees.

She didn't kneel often, since neither she nor James had much use for protocol, but the position came back to her easily. Butt on her heels with thighs spread as far apart as possible, her pussy visible. Head up, spine straight and shoulders back, with breasts thrust forward. Hands, palm up, laid on her open thighs. Chin up, and eyes down.

The last made her pause. James usually preferred that she keep her eyes on him in a scene, and if he felt otherwise, he'd either tell her or blindfold her. But there was a level of protocol to this scene that was at odds with how they normally played, and she just wasn't sure what he'd want this time.

She shrugged and lowered her eyes. If she was doing it wrong, he'd correct her, and since she could hear muffled footsteps on the carpeted basement stairs, she wouldn't have to wait long to find out.

She drew a deep breath as the footsteps got closer, then let it out slowly and forced her muscles to relax. She was a little surprised to realize how turned on she was already, and how frustrated. The open position of her thighs made it impossible to get any friction to her swollen pussy, and the cool wash of air over the spread folds was a delicate caress, a tease that made her yearn for a firmer touch. The urge to slip a hand between her legs, just for a second, was almost overwhelming.

Then the footsteps stopped, and the door swung open, and she didn't have time. But it didn't matter, because he was here.

She kept her eyes down, but her peripheral vision was excellent. He'd dressed as he usually did for work, in tailored grey slacks and a thin black sweater. His sleeves were pushed up to his forearms, his favorite silver watch glinting on his left wrist.

For some reason, the combination of partially bared forearm and the thick watch on his wrist had always made her mouth water. Which, of course, he knew.

He didn't look at her as he toed off his shoes and kicked them to the side. Didn't say a word when he walked toward her, unzipping his pants. Saliva pooled in her mouth when he pulled his cock through the fly, already hardening. He fisted it, giving it a couple of solid pumps, the silence stretching between them. Then he reached out with his other hand, shoved it into her hair and yanked her head back.

Her eyes widened and she jerked in shock, gulping back the cry that rose in her throat at the sudden sharp pain. Her eyes flew up to his face, which was harsh and hard and slightly blurred because, dammit, she'd forgotten her glasses again. His cock hit her cheek, a sharp slap that made her flinch once more, then he dragged it across her face to her lips and said, "Open your fucking mouth."

She obeyed immediately, the harsh words hitting like body blows, and saliva pooled in her mouth in anticipation. He shoved his cock all the way to the back of her throat, wrapped both hands around her head, and began to fuck her face.

Oh, my God. Amanda's hands clenched into fists on her thighs, her eyes watering as James drove his cock into her throat. This wasn't a blowjob—it was a skull fucking. He was masturbating with her throat, and the only effort required of her was to let him.

The *gluck, gluck, gluck* sounds of a wet, sloppy blowjob filled the room. Drool spilled from her lips, dripping down her chin and onto her breasts. She kept her mouth open and her tongue out, timing her breaths to his thrusts and fighting to suppress her gag reflex. He was hitting the back of her throat with every plunge, triggering a reflexive spasm that obviously felt great to him and scared the crap out of her, because oh, God, she didn't want to puke on him.

But she didn't, and gradually she relaxed a little. He wasn't going any deeper, and she had the rhythm of it now. With the panic receding, she was hyperaware of her growing arousal.

Her cunt was pulsing in time with her heartbeat, her excitement growing as he continued to use her for his pleasure. She managed to catch a glimpse of his face on the backstroke, and he wasn't even looking at her. He really was using her like an object, a thing that would help him get off and no more, and the realization was both disturbing and arousing.

Delightfully, frighteningly arousing.

She wasn't his wife now, the woman he lived with and laughed with and loved so beautifully, so completely. She was a vessel for his lust, a thing to be used. The thought reverberated through her mind, bouncing around like a ping pong ball as his cock battered her throat and her drool dripped onto her tits. She felt small, diminished in this role as his fuck toy, nothing but a receptacle for his cock. Small, diminished…and so fucking turned on she was stunned to find herself making the slow but inexorable climb to orgasm with no more stimulation than the cock in her throat.

Her clit pulsed, aching for friction. Her pussy felt empty, aching to be filled. His fingers dug into her hair, scraping against her scalp, holding her still while he plunged, retreated, and plunged again. His cock was like steel against her tongue, and every thrust pushed her higher.

She wondered wildly if she'd actually be able to come like this, without even touching her aching cunt. She wanted to shove a hand between her legs and fuck herself to orgasm, but though he hadn't specified 'no masturbating' for this particular scene, it was one of James' standing rules that she had to ask for permission. So she kept her hands fisted on her thighs as he continued to use her with no regard for her pleasure.

Fuck, it was so hot.

"Fuck, this is hot," he muttered. He dug his fingers in harder, jerking her head up slightly. "Good, fuck toy. Give me more."

Her eyes widened, alarm rising sharply when he drove in again, deeper this time, pushing ruthlessly into her throat. The muscle revolted, her throat spasming, lurching in warning. Panicked, she fought it, struggled to battle back the urge to cough, to vomit, as he shoved himself so deep that her face was buried in the open fly of his slacks.

"Take it," he muttered, his fingers tight on her head. She jerked in his hold, but he merely tightened his grip. "I said take it, goddammit."

She battled shame and bile as he held her there, smothered in his pants, his cock filling her throat. She struggled to breathe, to see, to *think* past the riot of emotions swirling through her. Fear and humiliation and dark, urgent lust tangled together in a messy stew, and all the while he continued to talk, the words raining down on her like acid, sharp and sweet.

"Fuck toy," he muttered, hips jerking as he fought to get deeper. "Come dumpster. That's what you are, just a collection of holes for me to dump my come into. If you puke on me, I'll beat you bloody, then toss you out into the snow. You hear me, cunt?"

I hear you, she wanted to say, but could only gurgle on his dick. Her air was cut off, her focus narrowed to the fight to keep still. The threat seemed huge and real, though the rational part of her mind knew he didn't mean it, that the threat was just part of the role, part of the game. But in the moment, in the heat and the mean of it with her lungs straining for air, it was very real. She fought against the panic, against her own body, eager to give him what he wanted so he'd give her what she needed.

More.

He jerked back, pulling free from her mouth. She sputtered, spraying saliva, her chest heaving and tears streaming down her face. He let go of her head so abruptly that she fell forward, off balance, landing hard on her hands. She stayed there, head bent, and continued to suck in precious air.

Through her streaming eyes she saw his feet move away, then he was back, his hand in her hair, dragging her up on her knees again. "Get up," he said, his voice hard and cold and impersonal. "Hold still."

She saw the flash of red in his hands, then he was fitting the shiny ball of the gag into her mouth. He pushed her head forward to buckle the straps at the back and stepped away again.

He snapped his fingers. "Get over here."

She gained her feet, wobbling a little until she found her balance, then followed him to the foot of the bed. Her jaw, already sore from the forceful skull-fucking, strained to accommodate the ball gag, and embarrassment rolled over her in a hot wave when she began drooling again.

He grabbed her arm when she stopped in front of him and spun her to face the foot of the bed. "Feet apart," he ordered in the same cold voice. She widened her stance, pushing her feet farther apart when he slapped the inside of her thigh. "Stop."

He crouched down, pulled something from beneath the bed, and placed it between her feet. She looked down when it bumped her heel, her fuddled mind struggling to keep up, and by the time she realized it was a spreader bar, he had secured it with clips to the D rings in her ankle cuffs. He attached a short chain fixed to the middle of the bar to the bed frame, then pushed to his feet.

She gave an experimental wiggle, rattling the chain. The bar kept her feet spread firmly apart, and the chain ensured she couldn't even shuffle a few inches to the side.

"Hold the fuck still," James said, his voice like an arctic wind, and his hand landed on her ass with a crack. She barely stifled a squeak and nearly fell onto the bed in front of her. She managed to stay upright, but her relief was short-lived.

"Hands."

She obeyed, putting them behind her, and felt him clip the wrist cuffs together. Then his hand was in the middle of her back, pushing her down so her face and torso rested on the mattress. She turned her head to the side, her cheeks hot. Her torso was slightly lower than her hips, so her ass jutted out, and with her legs spread, her pussy and asshole would be clearly visible, shiny wet with the lube she'd prepared herself with, and her own arousal.

The mental image made her cunt clench, and she wondered if he'd seen that telltale sign of her arousal. Then she stopped thinking at all, because he stepped closer, planted his hands on her ass to spread her wide, and unceremoniously shoved his cock deep.

The impact jolted her forward, pushing her hips into the edge of the mattress and forcing a grunt past the gag. He held himself deep for a moment, his hands tightening on her butt, then he pulled out and shoved in again. No gentle warmup, just hard and deep, doing what felt good for him and to hell with what felt good to her.

Just like he'd said.

She almost laughed—probably would have if the gag hadn't been in place—because as it turned out, what felt good to him felt fucking *amazing* to her. His cock felt huge in this position, thick and hard, exactly what she needed after feeling empty for so long. Between the lube and her own natural wetness, there wasn't even a pinch of friction, just the smooth glide of hard flesh into soft. Every thrust was like a punch, but it wasn't painful. It woke her up, made her eager for more, and she would have begged for it if she'd been able to talk.

He released his death grip on her ass and slapped both cheeks, one right after the other, getting her attention. "Tighten up that cunt, fuck toy. It feels like I'm fucking a sloppy wet sock."

Wet sock, my ass, she thought. *You love me sloppy wet.* But this was the game, so she clamped down on his invading length as best she could. But the spread-eagle position made it almost impossible to tighten her inner muscles effectively, and after a moment he smacked her ass again.

"I said tighten." *Smack!* "Your fucking." *Slap!* "Cunt." *Smack!*

The blows were hard, making her wince and bite down on the ball in her mouth. She tried again, but it wasn't enough.

"Goddammit," he growled, anger finally breaking through the ice in his tone, and he smacked her harder. "If you can't even do this right, what's the point in keeping you around?"

Blows continued to rain down on her butt, sharp and stinging while the verbal assault continued. "You think you're special? You're not. Fuck toys are a dime a dozen, disposable. I could replace you in an hour."

He yanked his cock free and stepped away, the abruptness of it making her grunt with shock. She started to turn her head—he hadn't told her she couldn't look at him—but then he was back, jerking at her fisted hands. He uncurled the fingers and pressed them into the hot cheeks of her freshly beaten ass.

"Spread your ass open," he demanded.

Her fingers tightened reflexively, her wrists as far apart as possible in the linked cuffs, pulling her cheeks wide. Between the spreader bar and her bent-over position, she was already spread about as far as she could go, but she held herself open to his gaze, her cheeks heating once again with embarrassment.

Then came the firm press of cool silicone on her anus.

She flinched, an automatic reaction to the temperature and pressure. She recoiled again when he slapped her thigh, then sucked in a breath through her nose as he pressed the dildo in.

"I'll force it in," he warned her, his voice somehow hot and cold at once. "Open up that hole and take it."

She struggled to direct her attention to that tight ring of muscle, tried to force it to relax, but the stretch and the burn was overwhelming, the pain sharp and bright. When the head of the toy popped through into her asshole, she couldn't prevent the high whine that escaped, but he didn't seem to care.

"Take it," he muttered again, almost to himself. He slowly but inexorably forced the dildo deep, not stopping until the base brushed her cheeks.

"A temporary fix," he declared. "But it'll have to do. Let's see how this feels now."

How what feels now? she thought hazily. The sharp pain had faded, an almost uncomfortable fullness settling in, and her asshole fluttered with spasms as it adjusted to the invader. They echoed in her cunt, her needy flesh pulsing with flashes of pleasure that only made her want more. Then his cock brushed against her pussy.

James fisted his cock, allowing the head to brush against the opening of Amanda's cunt, his eyes narrowed as he gauged her reaction. Her eyes widened in shock, and her hips bucked forward as though she wanted to get away. He didn't know if it was purposeful or instinctive, so he moved slowly, giving her plenty of time to safeword.

Then her ass tilted up, just a fraction, and he grinned.

The dildo in her ass was taking up a lot of real estate, and her already snug cunt—definitely not a sloppy wet sock—would be even tighter. She was still struggling to adjust to the dildo, though she'd thankfully taken his hint and thoroughly lubed up her ass. Normally he'd go slow at this point, penetrate her vagina in increments with plenty of pauses that would give her time to adjust. But today, for this scene, she'd had all the time she was going to get.

Still, he was careful as he fitted the head of his cock to the soft, wet hole and pushed. He gritted his teeth when she clamped down on him, tight and hot, so much tighter with the dildo in her ass. He held his breath and pushed through, digging her fingers into her hips, not stopping until his thighs were pressed against hers.

"Fuck," he muttered. He pulled out and pushed in again, the pressure and heat making him shudder. The dildo started to slide free, forced out by the pressure of his cock, and he laid a hand on the flat base to hold it in place.

"That's what I want," he managed through gritted teeth. "That's the tight cunt I want." His orgasm was gathering, the pressure building, but he wanted to hold it off. He wanted her to come.

"Good little fuck toy," he said, searching frantically for the right words, the ones that would make her burn hotter and brighter, the ones that would help get her there. "Hot little hole, perfect for my cock."

She clamped down around him, muscles fluttering.

"Greedy little fuck toy. You like that, don't you? Like being a toy, a come dump, a vessel for my cock." He let out a harsh laugh, pounding faster, harder. "You gonna come, little fuck toy? Are you?"

She whimpered behind the gag, her lashes fluttering and her eyes rolling back as her orgasm hit. Her cunt tightened like a fist around him in hard, rhythmic spasms, and all he could think was *thank God,* and let himself follow.

When it was over, he sagged against her, locking his knees to keep from collapsing on her completely. "Hang on, baby," he murmured, and planted a hand on the mattress to steady himself. "Just hang on."

He dealt with the gag first, fumbling at the straps with clumsy fingers, cursing under his breath when he accidentally pulled her hair and made her flinch. "Sorry," he whispered, and eased the ball from her mouth. He watched her carefully as she slowly closed her jaw. "Sorry," he repeated, and wiped at the saliva on her chin. "Okay?"

She nodded, her eyes hazy and her breath coming in ragged pants. "I'm okay."

"Just hang on while I get the rest," he told her, and levered himself off her.

She winced when he pulled out of her pussy, and let out a gasping cry when he tugged the dildo free, but by the time he had her wrists undone and her ankles free of the spreader bar, she seemed to be breathing more easily.

He left her slumped over the foot of the bed to quickly strip off his clothes and fold down the duvet. Those tasks accomplished, he scooped her into his arms and laid her gently in the middle of the bed, then climbed in next to her and pulled the duvet over both of them.

"How're you doing, love?" he murmured.

"Good," she said, her voice a little slurred. "You?"

He swallowed the ball of raw anxiety that sat in his throat like lead. "Yeah."

"Wanna sleep now," she mumbled. "Can we talk later?"

"Sure, baby." He rubbed her back, soothing himself with the soft feel of her skin under his hand. "Go to sleep. When you wake up, we'll watch a movie and have our traditional Valentine's Day dinner."

"Lasagna." She sighed and tilted her head back to smile at him with sleepy eyes. "I don't have to make it, do I?"

"I ordered from Capellini's," he assured her.

"Oh, good." She snuggled back into his shoulder with another sigh. "Love you."

"Love you, too," he said, and held her while she slept.

Chapter Eleven

They spent the rest of Valentine's Day relaxing. When Amanda woke from her nap, James insisted on drawing her a bath, then bundled her up in the blue cashmere robe again. They settled on the sectional under a thick blanket and watched comedies until dinner arrived. Then they opened a bottle of wine and ate straight out of the takeout cartons, watching more movies and laughing.

For once, James was grateful that Amanda needed some time to decompress before talking through a scene. It had taken him a long while to get used to her need to reflect and process before talking it out, and even after all the years they'd been playing together , he often had to remind himself to curb his impatience with her process.

But this time, he was grateful for the delay, because he had no idea what to say to her.

When she fell asleep during *Galaxy Quest,* James carried her up and tucked her into bed. He went back downstairs and cleaned up, washing the wine glasses and silverware and throwing away the takeout containers. He double checked the locks, turned out the lights, then went back upstairs and got ready for bed.

When he slid in beside Amanda, she turned toward him, curling up against his side the way she always did. "Love you," she mumbled, still mostly asleep.

"Love you, too," he whispered back, and lay there staring at the ceiling while she slept.

* * * *

The next day was a full one at work, and he hoped the client meetings he had scheduled would be enough of a distraction, but any time he had more than five minutes to himself, his mind inevitably wandered back to last night, and his gut would roil.

By the time his last meeting ended, he was a wreck. He was struggling his way through a set of changes to his last client's blueprints when his phone rang.

He glanced at it warily, relieved when he saw Jack's name on the screen instead of Amanda's. Guilt made him wince, and he answered the call on speaker. "Jack."

"James," came the wry response. "Busy?"

James looked at the blueprints, and the changes that were only half done. "Not really. What's up?"

"I just thought you'd like to know, we got a new shipment in today, with some cases of that wine you liked."

James pursed his lips. "The French white?"

"That's the one. Want me to set some aside for you?"

"Yeah, thanks." James sat back as a thought occurred to him. "What are you doing right now, Jack?"

"Slogging through paperwork," Jack replied drily. "The glamour never ends."

"Would you be able to meet me for a drink?"

"Sure. You can swing by here, if you want. No shortage of drinks."

That was certainly true. "Is now all right?"

"I'll tell the receptionist to let you in and dig out the good scotch."

"Thanks, Jack."

"No problem. See you soon."

James disconnected the call and rose from his chair, rolling the blueprints and shoving them into a tube to take with him. He could work on them at home. Right now, he had other priorities.

* * * *

Half an hour later, James sat on the leather sofa in Jack's office with a glass of thirty-year-old scotch in his hand and spilled his guts.

"I thought everything was fine until the scene was over," he admitted. "I'd gotten her out of the restraints, we were cuddling under the blanket, and I was starting to go over it in my head, lining up my thoughts."

Jack nodded. "Y'all like to talk it out right away?"

"No. If it was up to me, we would, but Amanda needs time to process and think things through. Unless things go seriously sideways or she uses her safeword, we usually wait."

Jack nodded, his expression calm, his dark eyes free of judgment. "Go on."

"I called her disposable, Jack, replaceable. I told her she was nothing but a fuck toy." He paused to scrub his hands over his face. "I've never said anything like that to her before, ever. No matter how rough the scene, no matter what kind of infraction she'd committed. It's just not me, you know? It's just not us. But last night, the words just came out. And now I don't know what to do."

"Sounds like you hit a landmine."

"What?"

"A landmine," Jack repeated calmly. "You had an emotional reaction to those words. Any idea why?"

"I don't know." James let his head fall back against the chair. "Maybe because my dad left my mom?"

"Did he throw her out?"

"Changed the locks one day when she was at the grocery store, a week after I started college."

"Did he replace her?"

"Yeah." James closed his eyes against the uncomfortable memory. "He married his girlfriend—the one he'd been cheating on her with—the day after the divorce was final."

"There you go."

He picked up his head to frown at his friend. "It can't be that simple, can it?"

"Why not?" Jack tapped his glass with one finger, then pointed it at James. "You don't want to treat your wife the way you saw your father treat your mother. Seems simple enough to me."

James stared. "Shit."

Jack nodded. "Yep."

"Shit," James said again. "I was so focused on not crossing any of her boundaries, I forgot all about mine."

"It happens."

"It happens?" James repeated. "That's it?"

"You want more?" Jack rotated his wrist so the scotch in his glass swirled, glowing amber in the light.

"Okay, let's go through it. Was that the kind of scene the two of you had agreed to do?"

"Yes."

"Did she safeword, or react badly in any way you could discern when you said it?"

"No, but—"

Jack held up a hand. "Did you mean it?"

James dragged a hand through his hair. "No, I didn't mean it. But, Jack, I told her she was *disposable.* I all but threatened to throw her out into the snow."

"Because you got caught up in the moment, not because you actually ever intended to do it." He gestured with his glass. "You've been married for what, ten years?"

"Twelve. Married twelve, together for fourteen."

"Would you say Amanda knows you well?"

"Better than anyone."

Jack nodded. "I'd bet a case of this scotch that she knows you didn't mean it."

James stared into his drink, his gut still in knots, then looked up when Jack sighed.

"Look, humiliation play is tricky. You knew that going in. That's why you set up these scenes, to see how they worked for you both. Right?"

"Right," James agreed slowly.

"And you figured out that objectifying your wife to this degree, in this way, doesn't work for you. So, you won't do it again."

James waited, but Jack just sat back in his chair, his tattoo peeking out from under the open cuff of his shirt, looking like a dark, brooding angel. "That's your advice? Don't do it again?"

"That's my advice." Jack sipped his drink, his eyes steady over the rim. "I do have one question."

"What?"

"Was the fuck toy thing hot?"

"Yeah." James blew out a breath. "Yeah. That part worked, for both of us."

"Then you just need to modify it a little. Go with beloved, cherished fuck toy rather than disposable, replaceable one."

James considered that. "As advice goes, it's not bad."

"I aim to please."

James ran a hand over his hair, exhausted by the emotional turmoil. "I hate fucking up."

"It happens to us humans." Jack tipped his glass back to drain it and stood to pour himself another. "Are you going to forgive yourself for it?"

James found himself smiling at the blunt question. "Eventually. First I have to ask for Amanda's forgiveness."

"If you need it, she'll give it," Jack predicted. He held up the bottle. "Another?"

James shook his head, setting his glass aside. "I have to get going. I want to be there when Amanda gets home from work. Thanks, Jack. For the drink and the time."

"I've got plenty of both," Jack replied, and lifted his glass in a toast. "Good luck."

* * * *

Amanda walked into the house and sniffed the air. The scent of grilling meat hit her nose and made her stomach rumble, reminding her that she'd missed lunch. She slipped out of her jacket and boots, tucked both away in the closet, then padded on stockinged feet to the kitchen.

"I smell meat," she announced, and James turned from the stove.

"I wanted steak," he said simply. "Hungry?"

"Starved," she admitted, coming around the island to kiss him. "I didn't get to eat lunch."

He frowned at that, like she'd known he would, and jerked his chin at the counter behind her. "Start on that. This'll be a few minutes yet."

She turned to find a tray of cheese and crackers laid out, and two glasses of wine. She helped herself to a slice of cheddar, savoring the sharp flavor, then picked up one of the glasses.

"Are you ready to talk about it, or should we wait until after dinner?"

"You mean the scene? Sure, we can talk it out. I liked it."

James flipped the steaks on the range top grill, then turned to face her. "You did?"

"Well, some parts better than others." She set her wine carefully aside. He looked grim. Something was brewing under the surface, and she wasn't quite sure of her footing. "My jaw is pretty sore today from the ball gag, so I don't know if I want to do that again. Maybe we can stick to the bit gag from now on, that one's not so rough."

"All right. What else?"

She frowned in thought. "I liked being manhandled, and I liked not being able to talk. The way you were talking to me was..."

He tensed. "Was what?"

She shrugged. "It seems like the more detached you are, emotionally, the more humiliating I find it. So, it was pretty humiliating."

He nodded, still looking grim. "What about the things I said?"

"Oh, yeah." She laughed a little, remembering. "That's when it kind of fell apart, actually."

His gaze sharpened. "What do you mean?"

"Not all of it," she amended. "Some of it was great, like calling me a fuck toy. That was hot. I liked being your fuck toy."

She sent him a sly wink, but he was still staring at her with narrowed eyes. "What didn't work?"

"Oh. Well, you said I was disposable and threatened to replace me." She rolled her eyes. "It sort of took me out of the moment."

He shook his head as though he was clearing the cobwebs. "Took you out of the moment?"

"Well, you didn't mean it, of course," she pointed out, and picked up her wine again. "Even in that headspace, I knew it was just part of the game."

"You knew I didn't mean it."

She sipped her wine, eyeing him over the glass. "Was I wrong?"

"No, of course not."

She cocked her head. "You look relieved."

"I am relieved." He scrubbed a hand over his face like a man just emerging from a deep sleep. "I've been wracked with guilt all day."

"Over what?" she asked with genuine shock.

"Over thinking you might have thought I meant it when I called you disposable and threatened to replace you," he said, and his laugh was relieved. "I thought I'd hurt your feelings."

"You would have, if I'd thought you were serious." She set her wine down. "But I know you better than that."

"Clearly." He took a step toward her, then turned back to the stove when the timer beeped. "Dammit. Hang on."

She watched him flipped the steaks onto a platter and turn off the gas, her thoughts racing. "You really thought I was hurt?"

"I worried you were." He set the platter aside, covering the steaks loosely with a sheet of aluminum foil before turning back to her. "I guess I was the one who was hurt."

"Baby." She stepped forward and slipped her arms around his waist. "I'm sorry."

"Not your fault," he mumbled into her neck, his arms tight around her. "I was so caught up in making it good for you that I forgot to consider my own boundaries."

She rubbed her hands over his back, eager to soothe. "Well. That must've sucked."

He laughed a little and planted a kiss on her shoulder. "To say the least."

"Why didn't you tell me?"

He sighed, his breath gusting over her skin. "I had to figure out what was going on first. And I was feeling too guilty, thinking I'd hurt you, to talk to you yet. I'm sorry."

"It's all right." She tightened her hold. "Did you get it figured out?"

He raised his head. "I think so. I swung by Jack's after work, talked it out with him. Turns out, I might have some shit left over from my parents' divorce."

"Oh. That makes sense." She laid a hand on his chest, a pang in her own heart at the thought of him suffering. "I'm sorry, sweetie."

He picked up her hand and pressed a kiss to her palm. "Thanks. I think I'll be all right. Jack was actually a big help."

"Sadist to the rescue," she quipped, pleased when he chuckled. "You should take whatever time you need to work through it. And if you don't want to go there again—"

"Apparently, it wasn't believable, anyway," he said wryly, and smiled when she laughed. "But I'd like to do it again. I thought it was one of the hottest scenes we've ever done."

"I did, too," she admitted.

"And now that I know what the landmine is and where," he continued, "I think I'll be able to avoid it in the future. And Jack had some ideas about how we could keep the good parts of the scene without revisiting the bad."

"Well, Jack is just all kinds of helpful these days, isn't he?" She arched an eyebrow when he grinned. "And speaking of the scene, and things that should not be repeated...sloppy wet sock?"

He ran his tongue over his teeth, eyes dancing with humor. "That wasn't hot?"

She snorted, delighted when he laughed. "You need some new material," she told him. "That's twice now that you've made reference to my pussy being 'stretched out' or 'sloppy', and not only is it physiologically inaccurate, but it smacks of toxic masculinity and misog—"

The words cut off when he kissed her, still laughing. "I wanted an excuse to put something in your ass," he mumbled against her lips.

"Since when do you need an excuse?" she mumbled back, and nipped his lip. His low growl sent a thrill shivering through her, then he took the kiss deeper, sliding his tongue along hers and devouring her mouth so thoroughly that by the time he lifted his head, she was clinging to him.

He rested his forehead against hers. "Next time I won't bother looking for one."

"Okay," she said with a dreamy sigh, and he laughed.

"So, all in all, how do you think our experiment went?"

"Hmmm." She snuggled into him, not willing to let go yet. "I liked the puppy play, but more for fun than humiliation. The public play was hot, and definitely humiliating. More of that, please."

"Okay." His eyes danced with amusement. "What else?"

"I liked being your fuck toy, but the threats weren't believable." She shook her head in mock reproach. "You'll have to do better there."

He nodded seriously. "Good note, good note."

She grinned, then sobered a little as she continued. "I think what makes something humiliating for me is when you're distant and detached. And I like it, up to a point. But it would be easy for me to feel abandoned if we took it too far."

He smoothed his hands up her back. "I think we have to find the sweet spot, that fine edge between not believable"—he smiled when she smothered a snort of laughter—"and too much. We can work on it."

"And we'll talk to each other if we're feeling guilty, or if either one of us uncovers any more landmines?"

He had the grace to look chastised, though he spoiled it a bit by rolling his eyes. "Yes, dear."

"Good." She beamed up at him. "I love you, you know."

"I know." His gaze softened. "I love you, too."

"Hmmm." She pressed a kiss to his chest, then cuddled against him. "Are those steaks ready?"

He twisted to look at the clock on the stove. "They need to rest for a few minutes yet. Wanna make out?"

She beamed. "I thought you'd never ask."

The steaks were cold by the time they got to them, but neither of them minded. They ate by firelight, feeding each other between kisses and sips of wine, then went upstairs to bed, leaving the mess for the morning. And when they finally settled down to sleep, tired and satiated, the last thing she heard him say before she drifted off to sleep was, "I love you, Mandy-girl."

Her "I love you, too," didn't quite make it past her sleep-fuddled mind, but that was okay. He knew.

Author's Note

James and Amanda use a product called Velvet Swing—or as they call it, "the good lube"—a cannabis infused personal lubricant that has the marvelous effect of longer, stronger orgasms. While I am not above making such things up in the name of artistic license, I'm pleased to say I didn't have to this time because it's real. However, due to laws governing THC, which is an active ingredient in Velvet Swing, it's currently only sold in California and Washington state. So technically, since James and Amanda live in Missouri, Velvet Swing wouldn't be available to them. But it's my book, and since I will absolutely use artistic license when it suits me, I've imagined a world where they—and anyone else who might enjoy such a product—can simply pop down to their local dispensary for a bottle whenever the mood strikes.

Want to see more from this author? Here's a taster for you to enjoy!

Perfect Taboo: Sharing His Submissive

Hannah Murray

Excerpt

Rebecca crumpled up the last bit of newspaper and tossed it into the box she was using as a makeshift recycling bin. "Last box, all empty."

"Nice job, love," Nick said, slipping his arm around her from behind. He kissed the back of her neck, his beard tickling her skin, then rested his chin on her shoulder. "Let's haul this out, then I'll order dinner."

She leaned into him and surveyed the unpacking debris that had taken over one side of the living room. "How about you haul it out, and *I'll* order dinner?"

"A traditional division of labor?" he mused. "Very Donna Reed of you."

"Donna would make dinner, not order in," she reminded him, and tried not to giggle when he gnawed playfully on her neck. "And anyway, I did most of the unpacking."

"Because you didn't trust me to put your stuff in the right places."

"True." She turned her head to smile at him. "But it still counts."

"Hmm." He narrowed his eyes, the bright crystalline blue darkening slightly. "I'll take out the recycling, but you have to eat dinner naked."

She forced a frown, even though her pulse began to pound in anticipation. "That's not one of the rules we agreed on."

His mouth quirked in a smirk. "It's not a House Rule, it's a Now Rule."

"A *Now Rule*?" she parroted, and frowned harder to keep the smile off her face. "What is that, something you get to invoke anytime you want something not covered by the house rules?"

"It's a spur of the moment negotiation for a specific situation. If you want me to haul all that away by myself, you have to eat dinner naked."

She eyed the broken-down boxes and wadded-up packing material that covered half the room. After a day of unpacking and arranging her belongings in his—now their—loft, she was ready to sit down and relax, and eating naked didn't sound like too big a price to pay to do it. But she wasn't going to tell him that. "Eating naked is dangerous. What if I drop hot food on myself?"

"Order sandwiches," he suggested.

She looked at him with a horror that wasn't entirely feigned. "Have you ever had breadcrumbs in your crotch?"

"I can honestly say I have not." He arched an eyebrow. "Have you?"

"Well, no," she admitted. "But I've had sand in there, and I'm guessing crumbs would be just as bad. I want a napkin for my lap."

"For a napkin, you'll have to wear a butt plug."

I'll need a napkin for under me, too, she thought. Her pussy was wet just thinking about him plugging her ass. She sighed heavily, the picture of a beleaguered, long-suffering submissive. "Fine."

"Fine," he echoed, and bent to capture her lips. The kiss was quick, with a just a teasing hint of tongue. When he lifted his head again, he was watching her with knowing amusement. "You're not fooling anyone, you know."

She forced her eyes wide and blinked, projecting innocence for all she was worth. "I don't know what you're talking about."

"Uh-huh." He slid his hand from her waist to her breast, where her nipple was trying to poke through her T-shirt. He gave it a firm tug, sending a quick bolt of sensation straight to her pussy. "You're sure that's the story you want to go with?"

"Give me a minute to think of a new one," she managed, and he laughed.

"Order dinner, then take a shower," he said, his hand light on her breast. She wanted to lean into him for firmer contact, but that would give him the advantage. Not that he didn't already have it, but still. "When you come back, bring the blue butt plug and the alligator clamps."

She was nodding before she caught the last part. "Wait. You didn't say anything about clamps."

"That was before you got caught lying," he said, and squeezed her nipple hard enough to make her squeak. His grin was pure perverted delight. "Infractions require corrections, baby girl."

"I don't think that's fair," she said, breathless from the spike of pleasure-pain.

"Want to make it a butt plug, alligator clamps, *and* a vibrating egg?" he asked, his fingers still tight on her nipple.

Shit. She shook her head.

"Then say, 'yes, Daddy'," he advised, his eyes gleaming, "and do what you're told."

"Yes, Daddy," she parroted, and bit her lip when he released her nipple. She couldn't decide if she was relieved or disappointed, and gave him her best pout.

It just made him grin. "Good girl," he said, and kissed her one more time before striding to the pile of boxes.

Rebecca shook her head as she made her way around the free-standing wall that served to separate their sleeping space from the rest of the loft, her body humming with arousal. It was amazing what that man could do to her with those two magic words. Sometimes she wondered if he could *good girl* her to orgasm, using nothing but his voice and the approval she craved to get her there. She didn't think it was possible, but she wouldn't bet against Nick, or the powerful, incendiary effect he had on her.

It might have been embarrassing if she didn't like it so much. But she did, and so did he, and knowing that made everything okay. Besides, she had the same effect on him—he was just better at controlling his responses. Hell, he was better at controlling everything… including her.

She wondered just how he was planning to control her tonight, and pulled out her phone to order dinner.

With the sandwiches on their way—estimated delivery time, twenty-two minutes—she stripped out of her moving-day clothes of yoga pants and a T-shirt and headed into the bathroom. There was a lot of things to love about the loft—high ceilings, spacious, airy rooms, and secure, covered parking to name a few—but her very favorite thing was the bathroom.

It was the size of the bedroom in her old apartment, and almost embarrassingly luxurious. There was a soaking tub long enough to fit Nick's lanky form with room left over for her, or she could just swim laps in it by herself. Two sinks on opposite sides of the room meant she didn't have to share counter or cabinet space, and while it didn't have a place for her to sit and do her makeup, she liked to do that in natural light, anyway.

There was a shower with rainfall showerheads in the ceiling that she could turn off with a touch on the state-of-the-art instrument panel when she didn't want to get her hair wet, and more shower heads set into the marble tiled wall. There was even a bench, wide and deep enough to seat two people side by side—or two people with one on the other's lap—and massage jets set in the wall behind it.

The matching tile covering the bathroom floor was heated, the lights under the cabinet edges motion activated so she never stumbled in the dark, and, best of all, the toilet was in its own separate frosted-glass-enclosed room. Not that she was particularly embarrassed by bodily functions, but sometimes a body needed to sit for a spell.

And on those occasions, it was really nice to be able to close the door.

She handled those bodily functions first, then stepped into the shower and tapped the wall panel to activate the rain showerheads. Moving day had left her feeling grimy, and even though it was still cold outside, she'd worked up a sweat. She might have lingered in the shower, letting the jets and hot water wash away the dirt and soothe sore muscles, but her stomach felt like it was trying to eat itself. Lunch had been several hours of physical labor earlier, and she was hungry.

She cleaned up quickly, washing her hair and scrubbing the sweat from her skin, then grabbed a fluffy towel to dry off. She wrapped it around her hair to soak up the excess water and keep it out of her way while she slathered on moisturizer, then hung it over the heated towel rack and dragged a comb though her long dark locks. They were getting to the long-enough-to-be-annoying stage, and she made a mental note to schedule a trim. She'd taken Monday off, assuming she'd be tired from a weekend of moving and organizing, so maybe she'd see if her stylist could squeeze her in.

She left her hair down to air dry and pulled on her robe. A moving-in present from Nick, the thick cashmere was soft, warm, and killer, fuck-me red. He'd said it had caught his eye because it was the exact color of her favorite lipstick, the one she always wore when she wanted an extra boost of confidence. She'd worn the lip color a lot in the three years she'd worked for Nick, and apparently, he'd become somewhat obsessed with it.

She didn't work for him anymore, and she rarely needed a boost of confidence these days, but she still wore the lipstick. It had a delightfully predictable effect on her lover, one that usually ended in multiple orgasms for her.

She debated putting some on now, but decided it was too much trouble. She left the bedroom on bare feet and crossed the bedroom to Nick's side of the bed. He kept the toys they used most frequently in his nightstand, the butt plug and nipple clamps she sought sharing space with leather cuffs, dildos and butt plugs in a variety of sizes, a rechargeable wand vibrator and a leather paddle.

There were other toys in the hope chest at the foot of the bed, just transported from her old apartment that morning, and in Nick's fully stocked toy bag in the walk-in closet if he wanted a more involved scene. But he liked to improvise, so he kept the basics close at hand.

She tucked the plug and clamps into the pocket of her robe, then shoved a small bottle of lube into the other. He hadn't asked for it, but maybe she could score some points by anticipating his wants.

She'd take all the good-girl-points she could get.

She walked into the living room just as Nick was opening the door to the food delivery, and the open floor plan of the space meant that both Nick and the young man in the doorway saw her. She kept her hands in the pockets of her robe, fighting the urge to draw it more tightly around her. The fact that it covered her from neck to toes didn't make her feel any less exposed, and the objects she carried only added to the feeling. Nick knew, of course. It was in the gleam in his pretty blue eyes, in the quirk of his lips as he smiled at her. And being Nick, he took advantage.

"Hey, baby," he purred, reaching out a hand in a silent order to come to him. She obeyed it without hesitation, her pulse pounding in her throat. "You remember Adam?"

"Sure," she said with an easy smile, her fingers tight on Nick's. "How are you?"

"Good, thanks," Adam said, his throat bobbing as his cheeks flushed. He was young, in his early twenties, working as a driver for several food delivery services to help meet his college expenses. Their neighborhood was his territory—if they ordered food, there was at least a fifty percent chance Adam would deliver it.

He had a small, harmless crush on her, which Nick found amusing. Rebecca found it sweet...and when she was wearing a bathrobe with sex toys in the pockets, awkward.

She squeezed Nick's fingers again in silent admonishment before reaching for the bag Adam held. "Thanks for coming so fast. I'm starving."

"I had them throw in an extra pickle, just for you."

"Thanks." She smiled at him, holding the bag to her chest. "I love pickles."

"I know," he said, and flushed tomato red.

She cut her eyes to Nick, who winked back and pulled a couple of bills out of his pocket. "Thanks for the speed, Adam."

Adam took the tip, his eyes widening a little at the amount. "Hey, thanks Mr. Saint, Ms. McBride."

"See you next time, Adam," Rebecca said with a little wave as Nick closed the door. As soon as it was shut, she shook her head at Nick. "You're terrible."

Nick merely grinned. "Seeing you in that red robe probably made his day. If you'd come out naked, he'd probably pass out."

She rolled her eyes and headed for the kitchen. "Good thing I'm not going to do that, then, isn't it?"

He took the bag from her and unpacked it, setting the sandwiches, chips, and pickles—two for her, one for him—on the plates she laid out. "And if I told you to?"

She pulled a couple of bottles of beer out of the fridge and met his raised eyebrow with one of her own. "Involving other people in a scene who have not explicitly consented to being involved in said scene falls under the heading of Things I Will Use My Safeword For."

"God, I love it when you get prissy." He grinned and smacked her ass. "Reminds me of all those times I wanted to bend you over my desk and fuck the sass right out of you."

She resisted the urge to rub her stinging butt and scooped up her plate. They didn't have a dining room table yet, because Nick had never seen the need and her old place hadn't had room. They were going to go shopping for one together, but in the meantime, their dining options were the living room or the breakfast bar. "Where do you want to eat?"

"Living room," he decided, and followed her over.

She was lowering herself to the sofa when he said, "Don't sit."

She glanced down, thinking she might have been about to sit on the television remote, but there was nothing there. "Why?"

"Because." He set his own food on the coffee table, grabbed one of the pillows from the corner of the sectional, and tossed it on the floor at her feet.

Her belly fluttered as she contemplated the cushion on the floor. "This is new."

About the Author

Hannah has been reading romance novels since she was young enough to have to hide them from her mother. She lives in the Pacific Northwest with her husband—former Special Forces and an OR nurse who writes sci-fi fantasy and acts as In-House Expert on matters pertaining to weapons, tactics, the military, medical conditions and How Dudes Think—and their daughter, who takes after her father.

Hannah loves to hear from readers. You can find her contact information, website details and author profile page at https://www.totallybound.com

www.ingramcontent.com/pod-product-compliance
Lightning Source LLC
LaVergne TN
LVHW090939080826
845145LV00003B/816

* 9 7 8 1 8 3 9 4 3 9 8 8 9 *